THE PRINCE'S CHAMBERMAID

THE PRINCE'S CHAMBERMAID

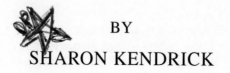

BY

SHARON KENDRICK

First published in Great Britain 2009
Large Print edition 2010
Harlequin Mills & Boon Limited,
Eton House, 18-24 Paradise Road,
Richmond, Surrey TW9 1SR

© Sharon Kendrick 2009

ISBN: 978 0 263 21205 1

Harlequin Mills & Boon policy is to use papers that are natural, renewable and recyclable products and made from wood grown in sustainable forests. The logging and manufacturing process conform to the legal environmental regulations of the country of origin.

Printed and bound in Great Britain
by CPI Antony Rowe, Chippenham, Wiltshire

To Judy Hutson, Catriona Smith and Narell Thomas,
who were there at this story's inception and who
inspired me—as did the green fields of West Sussex
and the wild splendour of Cornwall.

And to Rachel Thomas
for her invaluable research on head-hunting.

CHAPTER ONE

FOR a moment she thought she must have misheard him. Either that, or she was going crazy. And maybe she was. For hadn't her foolish dreams of love just been dealt a death-blow in time-honoured fashion? From her position behind the reception desk where she was covering for the receptionist's lunch-break, Cathy stared up at her boss in disbelief and tried not to think about the crumpled-up letter which was lying in the bottom of her handbag. Or the battering to her self-esteem which had left her feeling lonely, and wounded.

'Sorry.' She cleared her throat, wondering if he was having some kind of joke at her expense. 'For a minute then, I thought you said—'

'A prince? Yes, I did.' Rupert's smirk was supercilious, his upper-crust English accent even more pronounced than usual, as he paused to allow the significance of his statement to sink in. 'A royal prince is going to be gracing our hotel with his presence—what do you think of that, Cathy?'

'A *prince*?' Cathy echoed in disbelief.

Rupert's smirk became even more pronounced. 'Prince Xaviero of Zaffirinthos. I don't suppose you've heard of him?'

Cathy bit back the defensive response which sprang to her lips. Just because she was a chambermaid who'd never really qualified for anything didn't mean that she was a complete write-off, did it? The implication being that such a woman would barely recognise the name of a member of the English royal family—let alone a rather more obscure foreign version. But Rupert was right, damn him. Despite doing her best to keep up with world events via newspapers and books, it seemed that Zaffirinthos had somehow slipped off her radar. 'N-no,' she answered uncertainly. 'No, I haven't.'

'Then let me enlighten you. He's next in line

to an island kingdom, a world-class polo player—and a lover of beautiful women,' said Rupert, puffing out his chest. 'In fact, the most glittering VIP we've ever had.'

Cathy stared at him, screwing up her eyes in confusion because something didn't make sense. They both knew that important guests were few and far between—despite the fact that there was a world-famous polo club nearby as well as some pretty impressive stud farms. But there were also other, more upmarket hotels and she couldn't imagine why on earth a *prince* would choose to stay somewhere like this. Yes, the building was listed and yes, originally it had been a very elegant private home before it had been turned into a hotel. But Rupert's general mismanagement and dwindling guest numbers had left house and grounds in a pretty run-down condition, which didn't tend to attract VIPs.

'But why?' she questioned. 'I mean, why's he coming *here*?'

Rupert's smile disappeared as quickly as a ray of April sunshine. '*Why* is none of your business,' he snapped back, but then seemed to relent—glancing round to check that the coast was clear and paying lip-service to discretion, but clearly busting to tell someone. 'Well, keep it to yourself—but he's moving over here from his home in New York and he's about to complete the purchase of the Greenhill Polo Club.'

Cathy's eyes opened wider. She thought of the acres of valuable real estate which housed the prestigious club, which brought international celebrities flocking there every weekend during the polo season. 'A place like that would cost an absolute *fortune* to buy,' she said slowly.

'For once, you're right, Cathy—but that won't be a problem, not in this case. You see, this man is not just any old prince—with genuine blue blood coursing around in his veins—he also happens to be outrageously wealthy.' Rupert's eyes narrowed calculatingly. 'Which is why there are going to have to be some changes made before he and his entourage arrive.'

Cathy had been working for Rupert long enough to know just when to sense trouble.

'Changes?' she said, hoping that she was hiding the instinctive alarm which sprang up inside her. 'What kind of changes?'

'Well, for a start—we're going to have to spruce up the public rooms to accommodate a man of his calibre. They'll all need a lick of paint—especially the downstairs washrooms. I've organised for a firm of decorators to come in and start work first thing tomorrow morning.'

Cathy stared at him. 'That quickly?'

'Yes, that quickly. Someone will be in later to measure up—and you'll need to show him around,' said Rupert testily. 'The Prince will be arriving next week and there's a lot to be done between now and then if it's to meet royal expectations. Apparently, he only sleeps on Egyptian cotton sheets—so I'm going to have to send to London for those. Oh, and one other thing.'

His eyes roved over her in a manner she had always found offensive, but Cathy had learnt to ignore the suggestive way her boss looked at her, just as she had learnt to ignore his other annoying traits. Because no job in the world was perfect.

Nothing was. Everyone knew that. 'What?' she questioned apprehensively.

'You'll need to do something about your appearance. All of the staff need some sort of overhaul, but you need it more than most, Cathy.'

It was a criticism he had levelled at her more than once. But Cathy never really had the inclination to use anything other than a little honest-to-goodness soap and water and to drag a brush through her pale and disobedient hair. Her chambermaiding duties meant she had to be up much too early to make a fuss and, besides, the great-aunt who had brought her up had been a no-nonsense woman who had scoffed at make-up—and had taught her great-niece to do the same.

Cathy hated the way Rupert sometimes made her feel. As if she were only half a woman. Why did he do that? *Because he gets a kick out of it, that's why. And because he's never got over the fact that you once rejected him.* But insecurity could sometimes get the better of you and she found herself asking, 'What's wrong with my appearance?'

'How long have you got?' Rupert smoothed back the lock of hair which flopped over his forehead. 'The point is that the Prince is a connoisseur of beautiful things and beautiful women in particular. And while I'm not hoping for a miracle, I'd like you to make a bit more effort while he's here. Some make-up wouldn't go amiss, for a start. And you'll be getting a brand-new uniform.'

Most women might have liked the thought of a new uniform but something in Rupert's eyes made Cathy feel instinctively wary. Infuriatingly, she could feel herself starting to blush—a slow heat travelling all the way down her neck and beyond, to the infuriatingly heavy weight of breasts which had always been too lush for her tiny frame. 'But—'

'No *buts*,' said Rupert. 'I'm the boss, Cathy. And what I say goes.'

Well, she certainly couldn't argue with that. Cathy bit her lip as she watched Rupert sweep out of the reception area in that over-dramatic manner of his.

In a way, she had been in the job too long—
and sometimes she wondered if she would ever
have the courage to leave. Yet familiarity was a
powerful tie, especially to the emotionally
insecure, and she had never known anything else
but this place.

She had been brought to this village as an
orphan—delivered into the care of her great-
aunt—a formidable spinster who had had little
idea how to cope with a grieving child. Cathy had
missed her parents badly—she'd fretted and
cried at nights. And her great-aunt, though well-
intentioned, had been unusually strict with her,
extolling the virtues of clean living, early nights
and plenty of book learning.

But Cathy had proved to be something of a disappointment. Not a particularly academic child,
she had achieved little in the way of qualifica-
tions except for a commendation for cooking
and a special mention of the contribution she'd
made to the school garden.

When her great-aunt had become ill, Cathy
had been happy to nurse the old lady—wanting

in some small way to repay the woman's kindness to her. And after her death Cathy had experienced that same terrible tearing sense of being alone as when her parents had died.

The job as chambermaid at Rupert's hotel had never been meant to be anything other than a temporary post while she decided what she really wanted to do with her life. It had provided an undemanding refuge from the cruel knocks of life. But the days had drifted into months, then years—until she had met Peter, a trainee clergyman. Friendship had turned into dating and a slow-burning romance. Peter had provided sanctuary, and gentleness—and when he had asked her to marry him, Cathy had said yes, seeing a simple and happy future spread out before her, with a straightforward man who loved her.

Or so he'd said. He had taken a job up north and the plan had been that she would join him at the end of the year. And then yesterday, the letter had arrived. The one which had destroyed all her hopes and dreams and made a mockery of all she stood for. The one which said: I'm sorry, Cathy—

but I've met somebody else and she's going to have a baby…

She was so lost in her troubled thoughts that at first she didn't notice that anybody had walked into Reception. Not until a faint movement alerted her to the presence of someone moving towards the desk. A man. Cathy sat up straight, automatically pinning a professional smile of welcome to her lips.

And froze.

It was one of those rare moments which chanced along once in a lifetime if you were lucky. The sensation of being sucked in by a gaze so mesmerising that you felt as if you were being devoured by it.

Dazed, she stared up into the most startling pair of eyes she had ever seen. Eyes as golden as a late-afternoon sun—all richness and lustre— but underpinned by a cold and metallic gleam.

Unseen beneath the reception desk, Cathy's fingers bunched themselves into two little fists. She was unable to stop herself from staring at the rest of his face—at arrogant, haughty features which looked as if they had been carved from some rare and gleaming piece of metal. At lips which were curved and full—the corners mocking and sensual. But they were hard, obdurate lips, too, she realised as an instinctive shiver iced her skin.

His hair was dark and ruffled, and his olive skin was faintly flushed, glowing with health and vitality as if he'd been engaged in some kind of violent exercise. Tall and broad-shouldered, his physique was powerful yet lean—a fact which was emphasised by the T-shirt he wore, which clung lovingly to every hard sinew. The muscular torso tapered down into narrow hips and the longest legs she had ever seen. Legs which were encased in mud-spattered denim so faded and old that it seemed to caress his flesh like a second skin. Cathy swallowed. Her heart was racing and her throat had constricted, as if someone were pressing their fingers against it.

'I'm…I'm afraid you can't come in here looking like that, sir,' she said, forcing the words out.

Xaviero studied her—though without quite the

same awestruck intensity with which she had been studying *him*. He had noticed the way her pupils had darkened and the way her lips had parted with unconscious longing. But he was used to having that effect on women—even when he'd just come from a long, hard session of riding, as now. Her stuttering response was not unusual either—though it usually happened when he was on official duty, when people were so caught up with the occasion and the protocol which surrounded him that they couldn't think straight.

The most important thing was that she hadn't recognised him—of that he was certain. After a lifetime of being subjected to idolatry and fawning he was an expert in anonymity and in people pretending *not* to recognise him.

His eyes flicked over her in brief assessment, registering that she was tiny and fair. And that she possessed the most magnificent pair of breasts he had seen in a long while—their thrusting pertness noticeable despite the unflattering white overall she wore. Too big, surely—for such a petite frame? His eyes narrowed in expert appraisal. And yet completely natural, by the look of them.

'Looking like *what*?' he questioned softly.

Cathy's mouth dried. Even his voice was drop-dead gorgeous. Rich, like dark sweet molasses and with a strange and captivating lilt to it. An accent she'd never heard before and one she couldn't place at all. But who cared when somehow he managed to turn each syllable into a poem?

Oh, for heaven's sake, she thought. *Pull yourself together. Just because you've been dumped by your fiancé, there's no need to behave like some old spinster—eyeing up the kind of man who wouldn't look twice at you.*

And yet she could do nothing to prevent the powerful thundering of her heart. 'Looking like…like…' Like what? He looked like danger, that was what. With the faintly disreputable look of a womaniser who had probably left his motorbike outside—and she knew Rupert's opinion about *bikers* staying in the hotel. *So get rid of him. Direct him to the B&B down in the village.*

And do it quickly, before you make even more of a fool of yourself.

'I'm afraid that all our guests must be properly attired in smart-casual clothing,' she said quickly, echoing one of Rupert's stuffy directives and embarrassingly aware of the mocking twist of the man's lips. 'It's…it's one of the rules.'

Xaviero almost laughed aloud at the pompous restriction—but why knock something which had the power to amuse him? 'One of the rules?' he repeated mockingly. 'A very old-fashioned rule, I must say.'

Cathy risked moving her hands from beneath the desk and she held her palms up in a silent gesture of helplessness. She totally agreed with him—but what could she do? Rupert was still mired in the past. He wanted formality and ostentatious symbols of wealth—he certainly didn't want people walking into his hotel wearing mud-spattered clothing. Yet Cathy thought of the dwindling guest numbers and thought that her boss could do with all the help he could get.

'I'm very sorry,' she repeated softly. 'But there's nothing I can do. Our policy is very strict.'

'Is it now?' he murmured as he stared down into a pair of wide aquamarine eyes. 'And you don't make any...*exceptions*?'

How could he make such a simple query sound as if...as if...? Her mouth drying like sand, Cathy shook her head, trying to quell the haywire nature of her thoughts, thinking that most people would be happy to make an exception for *him*. 'I'm afraid we don't. Not...not even for guests.'

As she shrugged her shoulders apologetically the movement drew his attention to the sway of her magnificent breasts and, unexpectedly, Xaviero felt the sharp stirring of lust at his groin. For there was no sweeter temptation than a woman who responded to him as a man, rather than as a prince.

Placing one lazy denimed elbow on the counter which separated them, he leaned forward and gave a conspiratorial smile. 'And what would you do,' he queried softly, 'if I told you that I was not here as a guest?'

Cathy's heart gave a lurch. Up close, he seemed to exude an air of raw masculinity which had short-circuited her brain and was making her breath come in short, shallow bursts. What *was* the matter with her? Struggling out of the befuddled haze of her thoughts, she realised that his answer hadn't really surprised her. After all, he didn't really *look* like a guest, did he? 'You're…you're not?'

'No.' He paused while he thought about who he would like to be. Whose skin he would like to step inside for a brief moment of complete freedom. It was a game he had always liked to play when he was younger—when he had gone away to mainland Europe to college—and it had always driven his security people mad.

For Xaviero—or, rather, Prince Xaviero Vincente Caius di Cesere of Zaffirinthos, to give him his full title—liked to remain incognito wherever and whenever possible. Anonymity was his rarest and most precious possession. He liked to play at a life that could never be his for more than a few minutes at a time. A world in which he was judged as other men were—by appearance and demeanour, and by what he said. Where chemistry counted more than privilege.

Didn't matter that outside in a bullet-proofed car sat two bodyguards with guns bulging at their breast pockets—or that a further two were lurking somewhere in the grounds. For as long as this woman remained ignorant of his true identity, he could pretend he was just like any other man. 'No, I'm not a guest,' he added truthfully.

Suddenly it all made sense and Cathy wondered how she could have been so dense. 'Of course! *You're* the painter and decorator,' she said slowly, her lips parting in a wide smile. 'And you've come to measure up the washrooms.'

Xaviero's eyes narrowed at her outrageous assumption—but he could hardly berate her for insubordination when she had no idea who he was! He had been about to deny her laughable assertion, but now she was rising to her feet and instead he found himself utterly captivated by her lush little body—and by the sheer sunny quality of her smile. When had anyone last smiled at him that sweetly? Or treated him as just a man, instead of a privileged member of one of Europe's richest royal houses?

En route from the polo club to the airfield which housed his private plane, he had called in here on a whim. The sweat from a hot, hard ride still drying on his skin, he had been curious as to how the place looked before it was made ready for his official visit. But now he wondered whether the hand of fate might have stepped in. Had he been guided here by some unseen and benevolent hand, to have sexual hunger awoken in him once more by a lowly woman who was completely unaware of his true identity?

'That's right,' he said slowly, doing his best to hide another sudden stir of lust. 'I've come to measure up the washrooms.'

'Right. Well, in that case—Rupert has instructed me to show you around.'

Xaviero smiled. So he wouldn't even have to deal with the crashing snob of an Englishman who set his nerves on edge. This was getting better by the minute. 'Perfect.'

Cathy could feel the skitter of her heart as his eyes drifted over her. She remembered the discarded letter which lay in her handbag and yet hot on that memory came the realisation that no man had ever made her feel like this before. Not even Peter—the man she had thought she'd loved enough to want to marry!

Was this what love *really* felt like? The thought flew into her mind unbidden, before she firmly sent it packing. *Oh, for heaven's sake, Cathy— have you finally lost sight of your senses? You've only just met him. You don't know him. He's a stranger who's clearly aware of just how devastatingly attractive he is. And if he's going to be working on-site there's no way you can keep dissolving in a puddle at his feet every time he flicks you that curiously arrogant glance of his.*

She gave him an efficient smile. 'So if you'd like to follow me.'

Xaviero tried to imagine how a painter and decorator might respond in such a situation. Especially one who was mesmerised by a woman's petite beauty. Wouldn't he flirt a little?

Especially in view of the way she had been staring at him—like a starving cat who had just been confronted with a plate of food. Was she as hungry for sex as he was? 'I can't think of anything I'd rather do,' he murmured.

His provocative words were tantalising—but they were daunting, too. Cathy came out from behind the reception desk and then half-wished she had remained behind its protective barrier. Because standing so close to him, she felt so… *exposed*…so intensely aware of his towering height and his hard-packed muscular body. Her knowledge of men was laughably small—but even she realised that this man exuded a sensual kind of aura which spelt danger. So what did you do when you encountered danger? she asked herself. You put some physical distance between you, that was what.

'Let's go,' she said quickly.

'Mmm. Let's.' Like a snake lured by a charmer, he watched the seductive sway of her body as she led the way. She really was a tiny little thing— like a pocket Venus—with those curiously old-fashioned curves which made her bottom look so eminently cuppable. He knew from ex-girlfriends who haunted the international fashion shows that clothes looked best on lanky bean-poles without any bust or hips—but he realised instantly that this was the kind of woman who would look best with no clothes at all…

Cathy was trying to walk normally—though how could she do that when she could feel his gaze on her back, burning into her like golden flames shot from a blowtorch? She made the decision to leave the washrooms until last—because how embarrassing would it be to have to stand pointing out the peeling paintwork behind one of the cisterns? Instead, she stopped in front of a set of double doors and, pushing them open, stepped into a large, high-ceilinged room.

'Here we are,' she said brightly. 'This is our formal drawing room—where guests sometimes bring their coffee after dinner. It…well, it hasn't been used very much lately.'

Xaviero looked around at the general air of neglect. 'So I see,' he said wryly.

The furniture was much too faded to be described as 'shabby chic' and a chandelier looked as if it hadn't been dusted for an age. Cathy saw him glancing at it with a slightly disbelieving expression and, to her horror, she noticed a froth of cobweb lacing its base.

'It's, well…it's a bit difficult to get to—even with a feather duster,' she said apologetically. 'I'd have had a go myself, only I'm slightly on the small side.'

Golden eyes assessed her from head to toe, lingering luxuriously on her petite frame. 'You certainly are. And presumably you're not actually the cleaner?' he questioned drily.

'Er, no—I'm not,' she said quickly. 'I'm…' She stared up into the man's gleaming eyes wondering if her next statement would make his interest fade. 'I'm…I'm the chambermaid actually.'

The *chambermaid*? Sweet heaven! Xaviero almost groaned aloud—because the image which sprang into his mind was of a bed. A large, soft bed. And her in it, rather than making it. That soft, voluptuous form sinking onto crisp sheets and him sinking right on top of her. It was the most powerfully erotic image he had experienced in years and he shifted his weight very slightly in a doomed attempt to relieve the aching at his groin.

'Really?' he murmured. 'That must be a very…*interesting* job?'

Cathy's eyes narrowed suspiciously. Was he making fun of her—flippantly discounting a very necessary job which carried with it zero status? And yet he *looked* interested. She gave him the benefit of the doubt. 'Well, it can have its moments,' she said truthfully and then smiled again. 'Honestly, you wouldn't *believe* some of the things the guests leave behind!'

'Such as?'

Primly, she locked her lips together. 'I couldn't possibly say.'

He laughed. 'A loyal chambermaid,' he murmured.

'Professional discretion,' she agreed. 'And at least it's a job which gives me plenty of free time.'

'I suppose there is much to be said for that,' he

answered reflectively, thinking that she would not have dared speak to him in such a natural and un-affected way if she had been aware of his identity.

'Yes.' She opened her mouth to start telling him about the magnificent grounds which surrounded the hotel and all the secret places you could find to daydream in. About the scented haven she had created in her own little garden, but then she changed her mind and shut it again. *Just go,* she told herself. *Go before you make a fool of yourself. Because haven't you done overtime in the fool stakes recently? You've just been left by one man—so best not frighten away another.*

'Look, I've wasted enough time talking. I'd…I'd better leave you to get on with your work,' she said reluctantly, though she noticed that he hadn't produced a tape measure. Why, he didn't even appear to have anything to write with!

Xaviero studied her. The most sensible thing in the world would be to come clean—to disclose his real identity and tell her that he wasn't some painter and decorator at all. But he wasn't feeling in the least bit sensible. In truth, he was feeling reckless and more than a little wild—a feeling which had only been intensified by recent events on his island.

His mouth hardened. Except that it was not *his* island any more, was it? It lay firmly under the rule of his elder brother now—it was *his* domain. The moment the crown had been placed on Casimiro's head Xaviero had felt as if he no longer had any real role there.

The year of official mourning for his father had left him feeling strangely hollow and empty— and wasn't that one of the reasons he was here? To swap his bustling New York existence and make a new life for himself—by purchasing one of the most famous polo grounds in the world, and realising a long-cherished dream to build up a training school?

He stared down into the face of the blonde, mesmerised by her pale beauty. She was so tiny, so delicate and light that he thought he might be able to pick her up with one hand, and hold her—like a small trophy. He imagined his big, dark body contrasted against her pale fragility.

Could a woman this small accommodate a man as large as him?

He felt the recklessness transmute into desire—and the sheer and potent power of desire after so long an absence took him off guard. His gaze drifted over her lips and their rose-pink softness only increased his sudden yearning. Lips as luscious as rain-swollen petals and slightly parted as she gazed up at him. Lips that were born to be kissed; begging to be kissed. Would she let him? No woman had ever resisted him—because there wasn't a woman alive who would refuse the advances of a prince. But he had never kissed a woman under the guise of anonymity before…

How would he fare as an artisan? Did small-town country girls let painter and decorators take immediate liberties whenever lust coursed through their veins? He saw her eyes darken. Saw the sweet, almost wary way she stared up at him. It seemed that they did.

'No,' he said suddenly. 'Don't leave.'

Cathy's eyes widened. For a moment she thought that she had misheard him. 'I'm sorry?'

'I don't want you to go anywhere,' he said unevenly, and his smile was complicit. 'Any more than you do.'

There was a split second before the fantasy she'd been nurturing ever since he'd walked in began to come true. As he began to move towards her Cathy felt she should protest, but no words came—despite the certainty that he was about to kiss her and that it was both inappropriate and unprofessional to kiss a man she had only just met.

But Cathy's ego was bruised—she had been left feeling bitterly hurt by Peter's rejection. The future she had imagined for herself was no longer an option and she felt empty and undesirable. When her fingers had tightened around her fiancé's letter, hadn't she imagined that no man would ever desire her again? And yet, now—out of the blue—came this.

'You don't want to go anywhere, do you?' he persisted, on a murmur.

'I'm…I'm not sure.'

'Oh, I think you are, *cara*. Just as sure as I am.'

Leaning forward, he brushed his mouth over hers and felt the corresponding tremble of her lips.

'You like that?' he questioned unsteadily.

'Yes,' she whispered back as the lips came back and this time lingered—and Cathy knew she was lost as he pulled her into his arms and began to kiss her in earnest. Because it felt as if her life had been on hold until that moment. Peter's letter had left her feeling empty and aching and worthless. Yet all her fears and insecurities—all that hurt and rejection—were wiped away by the sheer, simple power of this man's amazing kiss.

Xaviero felt her instant capitulation—she gasped when he deepened the kiss still further. He felt the instant and glorious response of his own body, and his mind began doing rapid calculations. How long before his security bleeped him? Time to lock these doors and push her to her knees and have her pleasure him with those incredible lips of hers? She was too *easy*, he thought despairingly as desire now became mixed with disgust—for Xaviero freely admitted to having the double standards of many men where women were concerned. But that did not stop him guiding her hand to the hardness at his groin.

Several things happened at once. Firstly, an alarm began to vibrate in the pocket of his jeans—a movement which corresponded with the blonde snatching her hand away with a little yelp. And somewhere in the distance, a telephone began to ring.

Through a haze of humiliation and a terrible unfamiliar aching sensation in her breasts, Cathy took a step back and stared up at the man in horror, her cheeks burning as the memory of his hot, hard ridge seemed to be imprinted on her fingers.

'Wh-what the hell do you think you're doing?' she demanded tremblingly, though deep down she knew she should have been asking herself the very same question. *Why had she let this stranger take such liberties with her?*

Xaviero gave a scornful laugh as his gaze raked over her swollen breasts—their tips now clearly outlined against her ill-fitting overall, just crying out for the feel of his fingers and his lips. Frustrated desire quickly became self-contempt.

Was he so hungry for a woman that he should resort to behaviour like *this*? Like some teenage boy who had never known sex before?

'I should have thought that was obvious,' he grated. 'I was giving you what your body was clearly crying out for and still is, by the look of you. Sadly, I don't have time to oblige you, at least not right now—although, frankly, I prefer my women to put up a little more fight.' His mouth hardened with a mixture of derision and frustration as he fought the desire to start kissing her all over again. 'Did no one ever teach you that when something is given so carelessly it loses much of its appeal?'

Cathy felt a wave of injustice wash over her. He probably wouldn't believe her if she told him that she'd never behaved in such a way with a man before and yet why *should* she take all the blame for what had just happened? *He* had been the one who'd started it—who had begun to kiss her with such practised skill that she had melted in his arms like a piece of molten wax.

'I suppose you consider yourself to be blameless?' she demanded, wanting to slap him around his arrogant face. But he obviously saw the itching temptation in her trembling fingers, because he shook his dark head, the gold of his eyes almost completely obscured by twin circles of black fury.

'Don't even *think* about it, *cara*,' he warned.

The thinly veiled threat brought her to her senses as a sudden and acute sense of shame washed over her. But it was too late for redress because, with one final look of frustrated contempt, the golden-eyed man turned and walked from the room without another word.

For several disbelieving moments she just stood there until, in the distance, Cathy heard the muffled sound of tyres squealing over gravel and she hurried over to the window to see two expensive black cars racing down the drive at high speed. Automatically, she registered the sound of their powerful engines, and frowned. Now where had they come from, and where were they disappearing to? she wondered dazedly.

Trying desperately to compose herself, she

smoothed her hands down over her hair before walking back into the reception area—to find a plump middle-aged man standing by the desk, wearing paint-covered overalls and holding a large notebook in his hand. He looked up with a wide smile when she appeared.

'Can I…can I help you?' asked Cathy—though some chilling sixth sense began to clamour out a terrible warning in her head.

'I certainly hope so,' said the man, in a cheerful Irish accent. 'I'm the painter. Well, the foreman—to be exact. And I've come to measure up. So where would you like me to start?'

CHAPTER TWO

STANDING in the small bedroom of her cottage, Cathy stared into the mirror and shook her head in mute horror. How could she possibly go to work, looking like *this*? Like…one of those women you sometimes saw falling out of the pub late on a Friday and Saturday night. The kind of woman who poured herself into her clothes without stopping to consider whether they might be the right size. Yet surely the dressmaker couldn't have got her measurements wrong when she'd been for, not one, but *two* fittings?

She did a little swivel to regard her back view, and shuddered—because from the back it looked even worse, if that were possible. The material clung to her bottom and seemed to draw cruel attention to its over-generous curves.

Her nerves were already shot to pieces and picking up her new uniform from the dressmaker's had only made her precarious mental state seem a million times worse. She'd put it on with trembling fingers but it seemed unsuitable no matter what angle she came at it from. Too small and too tight—the man-made fabric strained over the lush lines of her breasts and made them look absolutely enormous.

She didn't want to wear clothes which made her feel self-conscious about her curvy figure, nor to plaster her face in make-up—which she hadn't a clue how to apply properly. But Rupert had read her the Riot Act and so she had reluctantly complied—just as she had agreed to jettison her normal comfy flat shoes and replace them with a pair of heels so high she could barely walk in them. Beneath the mascara and lip gloss, she felt like a fraud, but one who was not in any position to object—because how could she possibly do that when she had placed herself in such an unwise situation?

Her boss was ignorant of the fact that she had behaved like a complete fool who had allowed a complete stranger to kiss her in a way that still made her cheeks burn when she remembered it. Only in this case, the complete stranger had turned out to be a royal prince. A guest of honour who would shortly be arriving with all his royal entourage.

A lying and duplicitous prince, she reminded herself bitterly—and one who clearly found it funny to unleash his potent sex appeal and to amuse himself with a naïve and stupid woman who had fallen completely under his spell. Playing games with commoners—was that how he got his kicks?

After he had walked out of the hotel last week it had taken only minutes for Cathy to work out that the man with the golden eyes had not been a humble decorator—but Prince Xaviero himself. A fact which had been confirmed by her subsequent heart-sinking search on the Internet, where his official portrait had flashed up in front of her disbelieving eyes. Yet the sternly handsome face which had stared back at her from the computer screen had seemed worlds away from the denim-clad man who had kissed her with such careless sensuality.

On the official website of Zaffirinthos Xaviero had been pictured dressed in some sort of formal uniform—wearing a dark jacket with several medals pinned to the front of it. His black hair had looked tamed instead of ruffled and his lips had been hard and unsmiling. And try as she did to resist, Cathy hadn't been able to help drinking in his remarkable beauty—before reminding herself that he had deliberately deceived her.

Dragging her eyes away from his portrait, she'd clicked onto the history of the island instead. Zaffirinthos. A beautiful, crescent-shaped paradise set in the Ionian Sea—close to Greece and at no great distance from the southernmost tip of Italy. It was rich in gold and other precious minerals, and the di Cesere family was fabulously wealthy—with property and business interests in just about every part of the globe.

With one final fraught glance at the unfamiliar image gazing back at her from the mirror, Cathy realised that she couldn't keep delaying the inevitable. It was time to go and face the man she had kissed so impetuously and who, for one stupid and unedifying moment, had made her heart sing. And then what? Pray that he wouldn't inform her boss that she had behaved so unprofessionally—and leave her to fade into the background with her embarrassing memories.

It was a sunny summer's day and a pretty walk through green and golden lanes to the hotel. Although it was still early, she could see a big shiny black limousine parked in front of the entrance and a burly-looking man standing sentry at the doors.

'I work here,' she said in reply to the rather hostile gaze which was levelled at her as she approached.

'Identification?' he clipped out.

Fishing around in her handbag, Cathy produced her driving licence and gave it to him and stood while a pair of emotionless black eyes slowly compared her face to the photograph.

Eventually, he nodded and stepped back to allow her through.

Bodyguards clearly didn't need much in the way of people skills, Cathy thought wryly as she made her way inside. But once she'd substituted her trainers for the dreaded high-heeled shoes and locked away her handbag she looked around—marvelling at what a transforming effect a little care and attention could have.

All the walls had been painted a pale sienna colour—so that the whole place looked bigger and cleaner. Cobwebs and dust had been removed from the chandeliers, which now cascaded from the ceilings like floating showers of diamonds. Huge bowls of flowers were dotted around the place, and they seemed to make the biggest difference of all. Blue irises and white roses added scent, beauty and focus to the down-stairs rooms.

Yesterday, she'd made up the bed in the Prince's suite with the pristine Egyptian cotton sheets which had been sent down specially from London. Smoothing her fingers over their crisp surface, she had marvelled at how much money Rupert must have spent on his revered guest. Soft new velvet drapes hanging from the four-poster bed had completely changed the look of the room and all the lighting had been updated. Even the ancient old bathroom had been ripped out and replaced by a spanking new top-of-the-range version.

She was just tugging down at the too-short uniform when Rupert walked into Reception, a look of immense satisfaction on his face.

'Has the Prince arrived?' asked Cathy nervously.

'He's on his way. One of his people has just rung me.'

She felt the quickening of her heart in alarm. She didn't want to see him. *Liar. You've thought of nothing else other than his golden eyes and the soft promise of his lips.* 'I'd...I'd better go—'

'Wait a minute.'

Cathy realised that Rupert's attention was focused solely on her, his gaze slowly trailing from the top of her head to the tip of her toes. And she found herself thinking that when the Prince had looked at her—*no matter how much her conscience had protested that it was wrong*—she had felt an unexpectedly hot kick of awareness. As if his gaze had lit something deep inside her and she wanted it to keep burning. As if he had brought her to sudden life.

Yet when Rupert looked at her, all she was aware of was a faint sense of nausea and a slow creeping of her flesh.

'You look fabulous,' he said thickly.

She made to turn away, but he caught her by the arm.

'No. Don't move, Cathy. Let me look at you properly.'

'Rupert—'

'Very nice,' he said. '*Ve-ry* nice indeed. What *amazing* legs you've got! Who's been hiding her light under a bushel all this time?'

She was saved from having to answer by the sound of footsteps ringing out—and Cathy sprang away from the contamination of Rupert's touch. But not before she whirled round to see the look in the golden eyes of the man who was coming through the doors towards them. A look as hard and as cold as metal itself and she felt a shiver of apprehension shimmering its way down her spine as his eyes iced over her.

She had mentally been preparing for this encounter ever since the Internet had confirmed his identity—but nothing could have cushioned her against the shock of seeing him in his true guise for the first time.

Today there was not a shred of denim or mud-spattered clothing in evidence. Today he could never have been mistaken for anything other than a prince as he arrogantly swept in. His towering height and awesome presence were both imposing and autocratic, with power and privilege radiating from every atom of his being.

And no matter how much she told herself not to stare, Cathy couldn't tear her eyes away from him. The dark grey suit fitted his body closely—its luxurious fabric skating over every hard contour and drawing attention to the muscular physique beneath. A snowy shirt emphasised the soft olive glow of his skin and the jet-dark ruffle of his hair. But it was the golden eyes which dominated everything—gleaming and dangerous as they raked over her with predatory recollection.

Cathy's heart raced with fear and self-consciousness. Should she curtsey to him? She had only ever seen people curtsey in films and her attempt to replicate the crossed-leg little bob was a hopeless parody of the movement. She saw the Prince's lips curve in disdain and instantly regretted having made it.

'Don't curtsey—I don't want formalities,' Xaviero clipped out—but the quiet fury which was simmering inside him was not because she had breached some unspoken code of conduct. No, it had its root in something far more fundamental than etiquette. The inexplicable had happened and Xaviero did not like it.

Because the tiny blonde had haunted him when he had not wanted nor expected to be haunted by such a woman. A *chambermaid*! A humble, low-paid worker whom he should have forgotten in an instant.

So how was it that ever since he had taken her in his arms last week for that laughably brief kiss, she had disturbed his nights and his dreams. Was it because she was the first woman he'd ever kissed under the guise of total anonymity? And, by responding to him so passionately, hadn't she somehow managed to explode one of his tightly held beliefs? That despite his undeniable physical characteristics it was the cachet of royal blood which provided his major attraction to the opposite sex. Yet the chambermaid had not known about his royal status and neither had she seemed to care. She had seemed to want *him*, and only him.

The memory of her hungry reaction had taunted him with tantalising images of how that pale curved body might respond if it were naked and gasping and pinned beneath him. And all too vividly he had imagined plunging deep and hard into her body. Night after night he had awoken, bathed in slick sweat and inexplicably aching to make love to her.

Was it simply a case of her having been in the right place at the right time to excite his interest? His jaded sexual appetite returning with an inexplicably fierce hunger and swinging at him with all the weight and momentum of a giant ball bearing crashing against him? How else could he possibly explain his sustained interest in her?

Hadn't there been a part of him which had felt the whisper of anticipation as his plane had dipped down over the English Channel this morning, knowing that he was going to see her again? Knowing that he only had to snap his fingers for the little blonde to give him exactly what he wanted? He had fantasised about her lips on his aching hardness. The plunge of that hardness into her molten softness. The idea of losing himself in a woman's body after such a long sexual drought had been almost too sweet to contemplate.

And yet all he was aware of was a crushing sense of disappointment because the woman who looked at him today was merely a caricature of the one he had held in his arms. Gone was her scrubbed and fresh-faced appeal—for she had changed completely. From being like a sweet, native flower plucked on impulse from the meadow, she was now the manufactured and forced bloom of the hothouse.

The lush breasts at which the ill-fitting blouse had merely hinted so alluringly were now displayed in a tight-fitting and too-short overall, which only just stopped short of vulgarity. Likewise, her petite charms had been vanquished by the wearing of heels as high as a skyscraper. And her eyes! He had thought them mesmerising in their natural state. But now they were ringed with make-up—their sooty outline somehow diminishing the effect of their clear, aquamarine hue.

She looked like a tramp!

He felt the dulling edge of disillusionment and yet surely he should have been used to it by now. Because this kind of thing happened all the time. People were never truly themselves in the presence of a royal personage. They dressed to get themselves noticed. They said things they thought you wanted to hear. They were puppets in awe of his powerful position and sometimes he tired of knowing he could jerk their strings whichever way he chose.

'Your Serene Highness,' said Rupert. 'May I suggest—?'

'You may not,' snapped Xaviero as his disdainful scrutiny continued, 'suggest anything.' He recalled the familiar way the Englishman had just been admiring her as he had walked in. Was she *his*? he wondered. Xaviero felt the steady beat of his heart, remembering how, on more than one occasion, men had offered him their women in their pathetic attempts to ingratiate themselves with him. Would this man do likewise?

His mouth hardened. And would he accept such an offer? Did not his ancestors enjoy the charms of the opposite sex if they were presented to them in the same way as they might be presented with a goblet of good wine, or a plate of delicious food? He flicked his eyes over the blonde— noting the small pulse which fluttered frantically at the base of her neck. 'Who is this woman?'

'This is Cathy. She's our chambermaid— among other things,' said Rupert, and then he lowered his voice. 'I can get rid of her if you like, sir, if you'd like to speak to me in private.'

Xaviero gave an impatient flick of his hand to silence him. The presumption! As if he, Xaviero, should seek the private company of such a man as this! 'And she has knowledge of the area?'

Cathy wanted to open her mouth and tell them to stop talking about her as if she weren't there.

'Yes, she has,' said Rupert, as if she were some kind of performing animal. 'In fact, she's lived here all her life.'

Xaviero turned to her then, registering the automatic dilation of her blue eyes in response to his stare, and he felt a slow beat of satisfaction. Yes, she would be his. And before the day was out, too. Because this inconvenient hunger must be fed if he was to be rid of it. 'Good. Then she will be my guide while I am here.'

Cathy's lips parted and she stared at him in horror. 'But…but I'm not qualified as any kind of *guide*,' she protested in a voice which suddenly sounded squeaky.

'So?' challenged Xaviero, on a silken drawl.

'Surely…' Cathy swallowed as she twisted her fingers together. *It mustn't happen. He can't* mean *it to happen*. 'Surely you should have someone who is properly specially trained in royal protection, Your Highness.'

Xaviero's suggestion had been carelessly made—it would have meant nothing for him to retract it—but her objection secured his determination to have her. By expressing a wish to make herself inaccessible, she had sealed her fate. For a man who had spent his lifetime having his wishes met, it was the almost unheard-of protest which always intrigued him. Suddenly, the eager little blonde was not so eager any more!

'How very thoughtful of you to be so concerned about my welfare,' he murmured sardonically, 'but I want a guide, not a bodyguard. And someone with local knowledge is always much more useful than one of my own people.'

Cathy flinched. *Useful*. He had called her *useful*. It was the kind of word you might use to describe the pair of rubber gloves you wore when you were washing up. A deeply unflattering description, but maybe that had been his intention. Had he chosen it with malice and care? She glanced over at Rupert. *Can't* you *do it?* her eyes begged him. 'And besides, I work here,' she said. 'I…I can't just disappear at the drop of a hat to be your guide.'

'Of course you can,' Rupert said, completely ignoring the silent plea in her eyes. 'The hotel is closed to other guests while the Prince is here—and I'm sure that someone else can sort out the linen! Cathy is at your service for as long as you need her, Your Serene Highness.' He smiled and an unmistakable warning was arrowed in her direction. 'And what the Prince wants, we must make sure the Prince gets, mustn't we, Cathy?'

Cathy felt slightly sick—because Rupert seemed to have reduced her job and her status down to something as basic as linen-sorting. How sycophantic he sounded. Didn't he notice the Prince curling his arrogant lips in response to his toadying attitude?

But there were more pressing concerns than the Prince's arrogance—because she had very real reasons for wanting to refuse to be his 'guide'. Fleetingly, she thought of his kiss and her response to it. A heady encounter which seemed the most highly charged of her life had been given an even more piquant edge once she had discovered his true identity. She thought of the danger of being in such close proximity to him and excitement warred with fear. What on earth was his motive in making such a request?

She risked another look, meeting the cool mockery lurking in the depths of his golden eyes, and realisation hit her like a velvet hammer. *He wants you and, what's more, he thinks he's going to have you.* Cathy bit her lip. *And in view of the way you acted with him—can you really blame him for thinking that?*

And yet, if the truth were known, didn't she want him, too—even now? Hadn't the touch of his lips and his tight embrace made her feel really *wanted*—her broken and rejected spirit erupting into life at the thought that such a man could desire her?

Willing the hungry clamour of her body to calm down, Cathy hoped that her shrug disguised the frantic pounding of her heart. 'What can I say?' she questioned flatly. 'That I'd be delighted?'

Xaviero's eyes narrowed. Surely that was not *resignation* he could hear lurking in the depths of her soft voice? Or was she merely playing a coy game with him? Trying to show a little decorum where last week she had shown precisely none? 'Excellent,' he murmured.

Rupert beamed. 'Well, if that's all sorted—perhaps you would like to come with me, Your Serene Highness, and then I'll show you to your suite.'

'No, no.' Xaviero's voice was soft as he flicked his hand dismissively at Rupert. 'Go and leave us,' he ordered. 'The girl will attend to my needs.'

Rupert hesitated for one slightly puzzled moment before he left the reception area like a small child sent out into the rain to play and Cathy was left alone with the Prince. For a moment, there was silence and she didn't know where to look or what to say. All she was aware of was the prickle of her senses and the wild thunder of her heart as he caught her in the cross-fire of his gaze.

'You look wary,' he commented softly as he reacquainted himself with the aquamarine beauty of her darkening eyes. 'Are you?'

She swallowed. Wary as anything—and frighteningly excited, too. 'Why would I be wary, Your Highness?'

'That doesn't answer my question.' Dark eyebrows arched in arrogant query. '*Are* you wary of me?'

There was a pause. 'Not at all,' Cathy answered, but she lowered her gaze lest he read the lie in her eyes.

Xaviero's lips curved into a speculative smile. Didn't she realise that desire was shimmering hotly from her tense and voluptuous frame, no matter how much she tried to disguise it? And yet the fact that she was trying to resist him was proving to be an irresistible aphrodisiac.

From the cold, bleak space which seemed to

have inhabited his body for so long, he felt the answering tug of desire.

'Then show me to my suite,' he commanded softly.

CHAPTER THREE

'YOU look different today,' Xaviero observed.

His words whispered over her skin like liquid silk but for a moment, Cathy said nothing. Her thoughts were scrambled and her senses working overtime as she tried to come to terms with the fact that she was standing in the newly decorated bedroom suite *alone with a royal prince*. How disturbingly claustrophobic it felt—with his golden eyes searing into her as if they could see right through her tight uniform to the trembling body beneath. And close by was a giant, king-size bed. A bed she had made herself…

His bags must have arrived earlier, for as well as a whole sheath of official-looking papers littering the desktop there were lots of precious-looking things lying around the place. A pair of gleaming golden cufflinks stamped with an intricate crest, a beautiful silver-backed hairbrush inlaid with jewels. They looked priceless and ancient—but even more dauntingly they were his personal artefacts, reminding her of the intimacy of their surroundings.

A robe hung over the back of a chair—its rich, satin folds cascading down like liquid silver. White shirts glimpsed through the half-open wardrobe door—and a riding crop, with a worn leather handle which was leaning against a door. Cathy swallowed down her apprehension and wondered how soon she could decently leave. And yet if she was being honest—wasn't there a part of her which could have stayed close beside him all day?

'*Very* different,' he murmured as his eyes continued their unashamed scrutiny.

Her heart was beating out a frantic rhythm but at least *he* wasn't aware of it and that knowledge helped keep her face completely expressionless. 'Yes, Your Highness,' she answered matter-of-factly. 'I have a new uniform.'

He looked at the buttons which trailed so enticingly down the front—and which seemed to be losing the battle to keep those magnificent breasts contained. 'So what happened?' he questioned unevenly. 'Did you gain some weight while it was being made?'

Cathy suspected that Rupert had deliberately told the dressmaker to make the uniform tighter—but she could hardly turn round and admit *that*. Disloyalty to your boss was not an admirable trait—no matter how much he might have deserved it. And neither was answering back this insolently rude prince—no matter how much *he* deserved it.

'None that I'm aware of,' she said woodenly.

Xaviero found his gaze travelling over her undulating curves. No, if she'd gained any weight at all, then it had been a complementary gain, because there wasn't an ounce of flesh on her which shouldn't have been there. Hers was not a fashionable shape, he decided—much too rounded for modern tastes—but it appealed to the primeval sexual hunger which underpinned the desire of every man. The biological imperative which subliminally announced to the onlooker that soft hips and full breasts equalled fruitful and fertile.

He felt his mouth drying along in time with the increasingly sweet torture of his tightening groin. Those magnificent breasts looked as if they should never be sullied by the wearing of clothes—and maybe he should do them both a favour by removing them as quickly as possible. She looked like one of the naked women adorning his favourite painting in the Throne Room back in Zaffirinthos—the one he used to gaze at with surreptitious longing during his teenage years.

Yet this woman was not responding to him as he had anticipated she would. Xaviero studied her with interest. Today she wasn't sending out those delicious *come-and-kiss-me* messages which had made him pull her into his arms without thinking. Her eyes weren't telling him that he was at liberty to do so again—in fact, on the contrary, she was regarding him with the caution that she might use if she had suddenly found herself alone in a room with a rather terrifying snake. And why was that? Especially when this time they were not in a public place. Rather, one which conveniently had a bed in it—and his guards would not disturb him unless he gave them permission to do so. What the hell was holding her back?

Xaviero's eyes narrowed. Unless she really *did* desire the man she had thought him to be more than the man he really was! A woman more turned on by a painter and decorator than a member of one of the most prestigious royal houses in Europe. And, inexplicably, this thought excited him more than anything he could remember.

'So which is the real you?' he drawled softly. 'Did I catch you unawares the other day, all soft and natural. Or is this…*showgirl* appearance your usual look?' Irresistibly, his eyes now strayed to the generous curve of her bottom. 'Maybe you thought that a prince would respond favourably to the rather *obvious* signals you're sending out today. Am I right, Cathy?'

He said her name quite differently from the way anyone else had ever said it—his tongue seeming to caress the first syllable as if he were kissing it. And even though she was dimly aware that he was insulting her with that sexy drawl of his, that didn't seem to stop her traitorous body from responding. It was as if she had no power at all over her reaction to him. As if she was helpless in her fight to resist him. She could feel the blood pounding at her pulse points and her throat seemed to have constricted so much that she could barely stumble out her answer. 'I...I would not dream of being so presumptuous, Your Highness.'

'Wouldn't you?' he questioned as he noticed the soft rise of colour washing over her cheek-bones. 'That's a pity. Because maybe I'm in the mood for a little presumption right now. Maybe I'm bored with the people who always bow and scrape to me. Who act like puppets and tell me only what they think I want to hear.' He glittered her a look. 'Because, you know, I rather enjoyed the way you reacted to me the other day.'

'Sir—'

'I enjoyed the honesty with which you looked at me and the unashamed hunger you clearly felt for me. The way you gave yourself up to that kiss and melted into my arms—that delicious body promising untold pleasure.'

Her throat dried. Hadn't she been trying to put the memory from her mind ever since? 'Sir—'

'Why, if that infernal alarm hadn't gone off, then who knows where it might have ended?' His voice deepened, enjoying the way she was trying not to react to his verbal seduction. 'Except that we both know exactly where it would have ended, don't we, Cathy?'

Please stop looking at me like that, she prayed silently. A way which was making her blood move like thick, warm honey as it pulsed its way through her veins. Making her stomach feel as if it wanted to dissolve and her skin tremble as if she were standing in a snowstorm. She struggled to find something to say, but the only thing which came from her dry lips was a strangled little sound which was barely comprehensible. 'I—'

'And there's nothing I hate more than unfinished business,' he murmured. 'So I think we'd better do it all over again, don't you? Kiss me again, Cathy. Only this time without stopping.'

His words both shocked and excited her but Cathy could feel her body thrilling in eager response to the way he was looking at her. Wanting to feel the warm brush of his lips against hers once more. Was that so very wrong?

Xaviero's eyes narrowed, her hesitation surprising him as he reached out his hand and touched the smooth flush of her cheek. He couldn't remember ever having to ask twice before. 'Unless there is something preventing us? Some commitment you have made to another man perhaps?' But he spoke with the natural arrogance of someone who knew that there was not another man who could not be cast aside in the light of his own wishes. The Prince's desire overrode anything. The only thing was that meant he might have to wait…and he did not *want* to wait—not when his appetite felt so exquisitely and unexpectedly sharpened.

Cathy shook her head—her pulse racing erratically. How could she think straight when he was looking at her like that? 'No. There isn't.' She bit her lip as she remembered the sense of aloneness and rejection which had flooded through her on receipt of Peter's letter. 'There was…there *was* someone. I was engaged to be married, but…but…'

'But what?' prompted Xaviero, eager to get this one last obstacle out of the way.

'He…he…well, it's over.'

Xaviero allowed himself a brief smile of satisfaction. Perfect. Absolutely perfect. A fiancé meant that she was experienced—but that she had been faithful, too. Had the man broken her heart? he wondered idly. And if that were the case—couldn't he, Xaviero, show her that there was life after the end of a love affair? And that she could enjoy the caresses of another man…

He traced the outline of her quivering lips almost thoughtfully, recognising that in a way she would be getting the very best and yet the very worst of a post-fiancé lover. Because he was undoubtedly the finest lover she would ever know—but she would spend her whole life searching fruitlessly for a man to equal him.

'So let's make love,' he said simply.

'Your Highness!' she breathed, even though she realised that her protest lacked any real conviction. The look of intent which had darkened his golden eyes was just too beguiling—the expectation that he was about to hold her too tantalising to resist. And the sense of burning hunger in her empty heart was like nothing she had ever experienced before. *Should she stop him?* Shouldn't she even *try*?

She would never know. Because now he was pulling her into his arms with a smile on his lips which made her desperately want to kiss him. To relive the amazing sensations he'd awoken in her the other day. Half-heartedly Cathy twisted in his arms but the movement brought from him a low and mocking laugh and she quickly realised why—as she collided with a rock-hard and very formidable groin. She felt the mad, frantic race of her heart and the intoxicating fizz of her blood—her body blindly reacting to the sweet sensation of his touch.

'Sir!' she gasped.

'Xaviero,' he corrected, on a groan. 'What is it? Tell me.'

What could she tell him other than that this felt like heaven itself? As if she'd never been properly alive before that moment—because no man had ever made her feel like *this*. He was so close that she could feel the warmth of his breath on her face and it felt so unbelievably intimate that she felt weak. Already she was way out of her depth—and every atom of common sense she possessed was telling her to get away from him before it was too late. But common sense was immediately scrambled into a hot and senseless desire as his lips came down to meet hers—and Cathy knew she was lost.

His last kiss had been lazy, almost careless—like someone dipping a toe into a pool of water to test the temperature. But not today. Today it was as if he had dived straight in. His lips were seeking. Expert. Driving down on hers with sensual insistence and making her gasp with pleasure.

Without preamble, Xaviero pushed her down onto the soft bed, seeing her eyes widen in surprise as he began to unbutton her dress. 'You thought perhaps we would—how do you say it— *pet* for hours? The struggle on the bed as we remove first one item of clothing, and then the other? No.' He smiled as her milky flesh began to be revealed to him. 'I like my women naked,' he murmured and touched his lips to the pulse which fluttered wildly at the base of her neck.

Her thoughts struggled to make themselves known over the clamour of her senses. *My women*, he had said. Which implied he had known quite a few. She swallowed as his lips began to graze over the line of her jaw. *Of course he has known quite a few—did you really think that a man like this wouldn't have done?* Another button popped open and Cathy closed her eyes as she felt the whisper of his fingertip skating over her belly. Should she tell him?

But now he was sliding her shoes off. And her tights. And his fingertip was sliding over the insole of her bare foot—tracing a tantalising circle there—and Cathy thought it incredible that such a sensation could come from so provocative and yet so innocent a gesture.

'Ooh,' she breathed, forgetting all her misgivings as she thrilled to his touch. Because in this setting all the pomp and circumstance surrounding him had dissolved. Suddenly he was simply the man in denim again. The man with the golden eyes who had so bewitched her. Who was bringing her to life beneath his expert, seeking fingertips. 'That's…that's just *gorgeous*…'

Briefly, Xaviero smiled as he peeled off the uniform dress, briefly assessing her underwear. You could tell a lot about a woman from her underwear—and he had experienced more than his fair share of it. Virginal white lace—never applicable—or sensual scarlet satin chosen to send out a very specific message about the wearer. He'd seen just about every variation on black—and garments where less was supposed to equal more. He'd seen bottoms clad in French knickers and bottoms almost naked in Brazilian thongs. He'd seen stockings, suspenders and hold-ups, which always seemed to slide down at the most inopportune moments. But he had never seen underwear like Cathy's before.

It was… His fingers moved around her narrow back to find the clasp of her bra. *Functional* was pretty much the only word you could use to describe it—because it certainly hadn't been chosen with eye appeal in mind. Flesh-coloured briefs and a flesh-coloured bra—but then the latter had quite a tough and supportive job to do, he acknowledged.

But when the catch sprang free, it was Xaviero's turn to moan with pleasure as her breasts tumbled out, glorious and unfettered and free.

'Porca miseria!' he groaned, staring at them in disbelief before eagerly taking them in his hands.

Cathy let her head fall back against the pillow, vaguely aware that perhaps she should be objecting—but unable to form a single coherent thought, because now his lips were trailing sweet fire over her breasts.

'Oh!' she gasped.

His tongue stilled for a fraction of a second and

he dragged in a shuddering breath, feeling the jerk of his erection and the hot fever of his blood. She was as responsive as he could have hoped for—even more responsive than she had been in his dreams. And dreams were powerful things, he recognised—sometimes they intruded on your reality and altered it. So that for a moment he felt he *knew* this woman because he had met a version of her in the unconscious world he inhabited while asleep. Was that why he felt so intensely turned on? Or was it simply because his body was so hungry for a woman's touch?

Except she wasn't touching him at all—and maybe that was because she was clad in nothing but a pair of unattractive panties while he was still wearing his suit.

He lifted his head and brushed his mouth against hers. 'You will forgive me if I leave you for a moment?'

Cathy froze as the erotic bubble in which she had been losing herself suddenly evaporated. '*Leave* me?' she echoed.

Xaviero's lips curved into a satisfied smile. Did

they not say that low-born women made the very best of all lovers—with their unaffected passion and disregard for the convention that a woman must never be *too* enthusiastic if she wanted to snare a man? He began to trail his finger over her skin and felt her shiver in response. Because she would surely be aware that nothing permanent could ever come from such a liaison. Unlike the socially ambitious beauties of his past, this voluptuous little chambermaid would have no expectations of a future with him. And how liberating was that?

'Just while I undress,' he qualified, one lazy fingertip skating irresistibly to circle the heavy warmth of her breast. 'I want to feel my skin next to your skin.'

'Oh,' she said softly. Cathy's cheeks flamed with pleasure, revelling in how those simple words could thrill her so—her lingering doubts banished by the glorious reality of what was happening. 'What a lovely thing to say.'

'Well, then.' Reluctantly he moved away from her pink and white body and stood up. She was so sweet—too sweet really. He couldn't remember a woman ever being quite so straightforward. Quickly, he stood up, kicked off his shoes and socks and shrugged off his jacket—seeing the aquamarine eyes watching his every move, making no attempt to hide her expression of enjoyment. 'You want me to perform a slow striptease for you?' he questioned unsteadily. 'Is that the kind of thing which turns you on?'

Her cheeks suddenly grew pink again. *Perform?* Have the Prince slowly remove his clothes and perhaps have second thoughts about what was about to happen? What she *wanted* to happen. And *would* happen, she thought fiercely—because she had never felt like this before. Never imagined that this kind of expectant joy could ever exist—and it had banished all her normal shyness. Why, she was lying on one of the hotel beds, wearing nothing but a pair of panties, and she didn't even care!

She swallowed as she watched the Prince unbuttoning his shirt and revealing a broad bare chest. Up until now she had lived her life as she'd been taught—and where had it got her? Precisely nowhere. *And yet she had never felt for Peter what she felt for the Prince. As if she would die if he did not quickly come over here and kiss her again.*

Firmly, she pushed her conscience away— losing herself instead in the molten gold of his eyes as he pulled off his tie and let it drop to the floor, where it lay coiled like a silken serpent. She shook her head in reply to his question. 'No,' she said. 'I don't want any kind of show. I…I just…want you here again.'

'Then you shall have me,' he promised softly. 'Just as soon as I get rid of these…' His hand moved to his belt and then gingerly he slid the zip of his trousers down over his aching hardness. And then, after removing something which glinted silver in the light—something which he put down on the bedside table—he stepped out of his trousers. And his boxer shorts…

Cathy gasped and he smiled.

'So big, mmm?' he questioned with soft satisfaction as he climbed back onto the bed beside her and guided her hands between his legs.

Even though Cathy baulked at such intimacy, she wanted to please him—and after that initial touch she did not feel in the least bit shy. On the contrary, she was longing to know him and to explore him. To acquaint herself with every centimetre of his glowing olive flesh. Eagerly, her fingers tiptoed over the taut silken length—but he jerked away as if she'd scalded him.

'No,' he said fiercely, and caught hold of her hand, pressing his lips against her wrist and feeling the wild fluttering of her pulse. 'Not yet. Not the first time.'

She wasn't sure what he meant, but by then he had moved over her and begun to kiss her—melting away all her questions—dissolving everything except pure passion with the power of his kiss. It was…it was the most wonderful thing which had ever happened to her—as if she hadn't lived properly until that moment.

'Oh,' she moaned, her body moving restlessly beneath his as she silently communicated her growing desire.

Xaviero reached down to test her honeyed

warmth, feeling her buck beneath his fingers—
thinking how passionate she was. Usually, he
liked to run through an entire repertoire of his
considerable sensual skills—something which
completely captivated all his lovers. Women
thought him unselfish, and in many ways he
was—although he was always accused of holding
back emotionally. But he was aware that giving
them so much pleasure was also a kind of sexual
boast—an innate need to surpass every other man
that they might have known. For wasn't it the
curse of the younger royal son to always feel the
need to prove himself, in every sphere?

Yet as Cathy's fingers kneaded softly at his
shoulders and she grazed her lips over his nipple
he felt himself shudder and knew he could not
wait. Her fresh eagerness was like nothing he'd
ever felt before—like fasting for days in the fierce
heat of the sun and then suddenly finding a long,
cool drink of something indescribably sweet.

He reached for a condom and began to slide it
on, aware that she was watching him. If there
was one thing which had been drummed into

him since he had first entered puberty—it was the precious nature of royal seed.

Cathy bit her lip. Should she tell him how gauche she really was—and that she was terrified of disappointing him? But who in their right mind would want to let reality intrude and threaten this delicate magic he had woven over her? And then he pulled her back in his arms and began kissing her again, and it was too late to say anything.

She felt herself shiver as his tongue slid inside her mouth and that irresistible heat began to creep over her body once more, dissolving all thoughts in its wake. It was as if something had taken hold of her. Some urge. Some desire. Some *need* to feel him closer than close. Something beyond her control, which was orchestrating her movements.

She felt him suddenly tense as he shifted his position, his fingers parting her legs, and Cathy trembled as his mouth continued its heavenly plunder. There was a split second where one final consideration struggled to make itself heard and her lips parted to tell him. But it coincided with a single thrust, the sharp sense of pain mingled with the sweet sensation of this beautiful man filling her. Her strangled cry. And then his.

What was he saying? Surely not, 'no'? *No?*

Something had changed. There was movement, yes—but the mood in that bedroom seemed to have shifted inexplicably from joy to anger. Yes, anger. Bewilderedly, Cathy struggled to chase the incredible feeling which had been so tantalisingly close, moving her hips in time with his.

'Keep *still*,' he bit out.

But it was too late. She writhed beneath him with an abandon which was driving him wild, and that—combined with her hot tightness— meant that he was lost. Completely lost.

It was the most intense orgasm he had ever experienced and yet he hated her for every gasping second of it, withdrawing from her just as soon as his body recovered its strength from those powerful spasms. Staring down at her as a heavy kind of blackness enveloped him.

'Why did you keep something like that to yourself?' he accused, getting off the bed and grabbing his robe, before knotting it viciously at the waist.

All she was aware of was the condemnation which was spitting from his eyes as he towered over her like some dark avenging angel. 'But… Your Highness,' she said shakily—still not quite daring to use his Christian name—and her sense of shame and confusion grew, 'what have I done?'

'Done? You know damned well *exactly* what you've done!' he bit out with quiet rage. 'What kind of game are you playing?'

'G-game?'

'Didn't you think it might be a good idea to tell me you were a virgin?'

CHAPTER FOUR

CATHY shrank back against the pillows, her heart sinking as she stared up at the darkened fury of the Prince's features. 'I've done something wrong?' she questioned, her voice shaking with bewilderment.

'Wrong? Oh, please don't play the innocent with me!' Xaviero snarled, until the irony of his words hit him. Because she *was* innocent, or, rather, she had been—until about five minutes ago. But now he realised that a woman could be innocent in the *physical* sense while having the most devious of motives. And there he had been—imagining that she was a sweet little thing who had desired him as a man more than she had desired him as a royal. As if!

How could he have been such a fool not to have seen through her? To have realised that he was being lured into the oldest trap of all. Because she had misled him, that was why. And so cleverly, too—those big aquamarine eyes clearly concealing a scheming brain, that voluptuous body luring him with its seductive promise. His fist clenched with impotent fury. 'Did you lie about having a fiancé?'

'No!' she protested. 'I did have one!'

'Then how can you still be a virgin if you were engaged to be married?' he flared. 'I know that nobody waits until their wedding day any more—well, certainly not in the world which *you* inhabit!'

Cathy saw the contempt which had twisted his sensual lips, and flinched at how little he obviously thought of her. Oh, what a fool she had been. What a stupid little fool. Her greatest gift and she had given it to a man who had thrown it back in her face as if it had been a dirty rag. Her virginity treated with the contempt with which he might have viewed the bargain-basket at the supermarket. Except that she doubted this man had ever been near a supermarket in his life.

'As a matter of fact, he said he thought we should wait until we were married!' she objected heatedly.

'And *you*—a woman who turns on as quickly as you do—you were *happy* to wait?' he demanded, in disbelief.

'Well, *yes*! Actually, I was.' With Peter waiting had never been a problem and in view of his job it had been more than appropriate. 'He wasn't like you,' she finished miserably.

'Nobody is like me,' he qualified arrogantly, before his features darkened even more. 'I have been duped,' he grated.

Cathy stared at him. Wasn't he forgetting something? 'And what about me?' she whispered. 'You duped me, too, didn't you? Pretending to be a painter and decorator! What was that all about?'

But he was not listening, his mind working overtime—until the realisation of what must have happened hit him like a dull blow in the solar plexus. He thought of the Englishman,

Rupert. The way she had whirled away from him when he had entered the hotel that morning. Surely *he* was not the fiancé?

'It is this…this…*Rupert*?' he accused hotly.

For a moment Cathy stared at him in complete puzzlement. 'What is?'

'He was the man you were to have married?'

'No!' she protested, appalled. 'My fiancé was a trainee clergyman,' she added, though this added piece of information seemed to make him even angrier.

Xaviero's eyes narrowed. Then what the hell was going on—were she and the hotel owner colluding? Had he convinced this little chambermaid to seduce him for his own nefarious purpose? But there was no way he could possibly interrogate her when she was lying there so bare and so beautiful. 'Cover yourself up!' he demanded hotly.

Cathy wondered if he meant for her to start dressing and she went to get off the bed when something in her movement made his face darken again and he bent and picked up the silky coverlet which must have slipped to the ground during their love-making. *Love-making*, she thought in revulsion as she hastily caught the coverlet he tossed towards her, and hauled it over her body. The last word you could ever apply to what had just happened was *love*.

Xaviero drew a deep breath as he looked at her, at the pale hair beginning to fall out of the pins which constrained it—thinking that he had been so eager to possess her that he hadn't even got around to letting it spill over her magnificent breasts. A pulse flickered at his temple. 'Okay,' he said steadily. 'Let's just get it out of the way. Tell me what it is you want?'

'What I w-want?'

'You heard me!'

She stared at him. What she wanted was to be rid of this terrible feeling that she had just made the biggest mistake of her life. Or for the last ten minutes not to have happened and for him to come back and start kissing her again. But she suspected that neither of those options was going to happen. 'I don't understand what you're talking about.'

Xaviero looked at her disbelievingly. Had he believed those eyes to be so guileless, her passion to be so sweet, because he had *wanted* to believe it? But he came from a world where virginity was highly prized—an old-fashioned royal essential to ensure the pure continuation of his ancient bloodline. And he could not believe that any woman would have given it away so carelessly unless she had some kind of separate agenda.

'You must want something to have behaved so impetuously,' he snapped. 'Did you collude with your boss? Provide the irresistible bait with your too-tight uniform and your over-made-up eyes? Knowing all the obvious ploys which will hook in a man. Yet I *knew* all that, and *still* I fell for it,' he added bitterly. 'Because sexual hunger has made fools of men since the beginning of time.'

'I don't understand,' said Cathy again, beginning to grow a little bit angry now. Yes, he was a prince and yes, he seemed genuinely shocked that she had been a virgin—but everything was about *him*, wasn't it? Him, him, him! Didn't he stop to think for a moment about how *she* was feeling

SHARON KENDRICK 89

right now? Foolish and empty and aware that she had been carried away by a hopeless fantasy that there was a spark of something *real* between her and the golden-eyed man. Something which had begun the very first time she'd seen him. Inexperience had made her attribute the passion of his kiss to something more than mere lust. So hadn't *she* been the fool, not him?

Clutching onto the silken coverlet, she lifted her chin. 'Why on earth should I want to collude with Rupert?'

'To negotiate a better price?' he returned, golden eyes lancing into her.

For a moment the room seemed to sway and Cathy felt sick. 'To negotiate a better *price*?' she echoed in disbelief. Surely—oh, please, no— surely he wasn't implying that she was *selling herself*. She swallowed down the acrid taste in her throat. 'A better price for *what*?'

'For the hotel, of course,' he snapped.

There was an odd, debilitating kind of silence. A moment when it seemed to her that every- thing which was dark in the world had formed itself into a horrible, tight little ball and been hurled, hard—at her stomach. 'For the hotel?' she whispered.

There was a pause. 'He hasn't told you?'

'Told…told me what?'

'That he's selling?' His eyes narrowed as he saw her face blanch. 'No, clearly he hasn't.'

'To…*you*?'

Xaviero gave a grim kind of smile. 'Of course to me.'

Through the series of befuddled impressions which began ricocheting through her mind, Cathy's overriding thought was that she would have to leave now. She would *have* to. Prince Xaviero as her *boss*? How could she bear it? But then she met the cold, metallic gleam of his golden eyes and wondered who on earth she thought she was kidding. As if a man who had made his contempt for her so apparent would ever keep her on the payroll.

But something didn't make sense to her. She knew that princes in modern times had 'normal' careers—but *this*? She tried to imagine him doing a stocktake of the cellar—or taking the chef to task when he had one of his periodical tantrums.

'You mean…you're going to be a hotelier?' she questioned, mystified.

There was a moment of stunned silence before Xaviero gave an arrogant laugh, knowing that he should have been outraged at her suggestion and yet, in a way, didn't it make walking away from her not just easy—but necessary? Because her ridiculous question had simply confirmed that he could not have picked a more unsuitable lover if he had searched to the ends of the earth to find one.

'You can see *me*—running a hotel such as *this*?' he mocked.

Now he came to mention it, no, she couldn't—but something in his contemptuous attitude stabbed even harder at Cathy's heart. It might not have been the most fashionable hotel in the country, but it was the only real job she'd ever had—and she felt a certain kind of loyalty towards it.

'Not really, no,' she said. Because some modicum of politeness and charm were necessary if you wanted to make a place a real success—and, unless he was actually trying to get a woman to kiss him, the arrogant Prince Xaviero seemed badly lacking in both. 'So why are you buying it, then?'

'Because I want a retreat—a beautiful, English country home, which this has the potential to be. Something with history which can be brought up to date with a little care and money injected into it. Somewhere that's close enough to London and the international airports—near enough to my polo club but far away enough to escape from it. Somewhere big enough to site a helicopter pad—and which will satisfy my security people. This place seems to fulfil most of the criteria— though obviously it needs extensive work before it can be made habitable.' He began to laugh softly. '*Me*? A hotelier? Can you *imagine*?'

Cathy stared at him. In a way, she had thought the worst thing that could happen was the Prince taking over the hotel—but now she saw that there was a far worse scenario. That soon there would be no hotel at all—it would revert to being a private home and not just she but all the other people who worked there would be out of a job. Dismissed as if they were of no consequence by a spoilt and selfish prince who thought of nobody but himself!

'No, now I come to think of it, I can't—it was a ri-ridiculous thing to say,' she agreed, her voice shaking with rage and hurt. 'I don't think you've got the people skills to run a hotel.'

There was a stunned silence, while he stared at her in a slow-burning disbelief. '*What* did you just say?'

Don't let him intimidate you, thought Cathy fiercely—because now indignation was taking over from the terrible hurt which seemed to have turned her body into a block of ice. Had she done something awful in a past life which meant that men felt they had a right to trample over her feelings like a herd of cows in a meadow? He had just taken her virginity and then turned on her as if she were nothing more than a cheap con-artist.

'I think you heard me.'

'How dare you?' he bit out dangerously.

'Why?' She didn't flinch under his accusing stare. 'Does the truth make you angry, Your *Highness*?'

Xaviero's eyes narrowed as her impudence almost took his breath away. 'This is completely unacceptable!' he hissed.

Didn't what they had just been doing give her at least *some* rights? Clearly not. Clutching the silken coverlet even tighter, Cathy thought that if someone had spoken to him like that more often in the past, then he might not be so overbearingly arrogant. 'Well, if you'll let me leave—then I won't need to bother you any more, will I?'

Still reeling from her insubordination, he paused to study her flushed face and the aquamarine eyes which were unexpectedly sparking blue fire at him. And even while her sudden defiance began to turn him on he remembered something else, too. Something which might account for her spiky rebelliousness.

'I'm not stopping you from leaving,' he said softly.

She stared at him—as a hungry mouse might stare at a piece of cheese while wondering what the glint of metal behind it could possibly be. 'You…you aren't?'

'Of course not.' He smiled, feeling himself grow exquisitely hard beneath his robe. 'Go. Go on, if that's what you want.'

Cathy swallowed, knowing that she could not move an inch while those eyes were melting into her like molten gold. 'Then…then would you mind turning your back?'

His lips curved into a mocking smile. 'Yes, I would, actually.' He reached out and hooked his finger inside the silk-satin rim of the coverlet which concealed the trembling rise and fall of her breasts. 'Isn't it a little late in the day for modesty?'

Her breathing was coming in short little bursts. 'N-no. I don't th-think it is.'

The finger slipped a little further down and sank into the cushioned flesh. 'Sure?'

'Q-quite sure,' she breathed, wanting—no, *praying* that he wouldn't stop touching her even while part of her despised herself for letting him.

Push him away, she told herself. *Push him away and he will let you go*. Because despite the dark look of predatory intent which had made his features grow tense, some deep-rooted instinct told her that he would stop immediately if she wanted him to.

'You see, what just happened was not the best initiation into sex you could have had, *mia cara*,' he murmured as his finger dipped down and began to tease at one tightly aroused nipple.

Cathy's grip on the coverlet loosened. 'It… wasn't?'

'No.' His palm now captured the entire heavy mound of her breast and he felt the coverlet slither down uselessly to her waist. Leaning over, he bent his lips to one rosy tip, feeling a convulsive shudder rack her tiny frame as he flicked his tongue against it. 'If I had known…' *If he had known, he would have run a million miles away from her blue-eyed enchantment*. But perhaps this wasn't the best time in the world to say so. 'Then I should have taken things more…slowly.'

Cathy's eyes fluttered to a close as she felt his

tongue now slide its way down towards her belly, and an unbearable flame of desire shot through her. 'Oh,' she breathed as he slid a slow, moist trail over her skin and her fingers drifted automatically to tangle themselves in the dark silk of his hair. Sweet sensation sucked her towards an unknown vortex as she struggled to hold onto reality. She wanted to ask him what he thought he was doing—but it felt so good that she didn't want to risk him stopping by answering.

'Is that good?' he murmured as his mouth lingered against her navel—his tongue circling the neat little hollow.

Good? 'Yes,' she breathed.

Parting her legs with gentle fingers, he put his face between her thighs, his first slow lick producing a squirm of pleasure and a disbelieving intake of breath.

'Oh!' she gasped as his tongue began to move against her heated flesh. Cathy was on fire—as the growing hunger of her body demanded to be fed. And in a way, this felt even more intimate than what had happened before. The Prince kissing her there…there…how was that possible? But then she forgot that he was a prince, forgot the angry words and the accusations which had preceded this, forgot everything except the sensations which began to build and build, promising her some tantalising conclusion so perfect that she didn't dare dream that it might really exist.

But it did. It really did. She choked back a cry of disbelief, her back arched like a bow as it began to happen and she was hurtled, unprepared—into an entirely new stratosphere. It was like slowly falling off a cliff and into a warm and soaring sea—as waves and waves of warm pleasure began to wash over her.

Moving away from her, Xaviero watched her climax, unbearably turned on himself as he watched one hand stray to her neck, as if heating itself on the rose-bloom flush which had begun to flower there. For a moment he saw her naked body shift in lazy and uninhibited contentment, but when eventually her eyes fluttered open they fixed on him, suddenly becoming veiled, as if she was remembering exactly where she was, and with whom—and uncertain of what to do next.

There was a moment's silence.

'You liked that,' he observed eventually, swallowing down the sudden lump in his throat.

Still dazed and confused by the intense experience, Cathy shook her head.

'You *didn't*?' he murmured mockingly.

'Oh, yes, I did—of course I did.' She wanted to fling her arms around his neck. She wanted to cover him with a million little kisses of gratitude for making her feel that way, but she didn't dare. 'It was…oh, it was the most incredible experience of my entire life.'

He smiled. Her unqualified praise was rather touching, because all women thought it—even if few were gauche enough to express it so fulsomely. 'That is what was making you so…argumentative,' he observed reflectively. 'You should have an orgasm every time you have sex.'

Cathy cringed, the baldness of his statement shocking her—though not quite enough to pull away from his embrace—telling herself that at

least nobody could accuse him of being a hypocrite. And then her attention was caught by the
unmistakably hard outline which was apparent
beneath the rich fabric of his satin robe and as
their eyes met in silent acknowledgement she
found herself blushing.

'Yes,' he agreed, as if responding to an
unspoken question. 'I want you very much
indeed—but I have to be at a meeting in…' he
flicked an impatient glance up at the clock which
hung over the beautiful marble fireplace '…just
under an hour…' his voice lowered '…which
means there won't be enough time.'

He thought that if she had been more experienced there would have been plenty of time. By
now she would have taken the initiative and he
would have loved nothing more than to see her
on her knees in front of him. Pleasuring him with
her lips while he tangled his fingers in the pale
silk of her hair and fulfilled the very first fantasy
he'd ever had about her.

And that was when a solution presented itself
to him—a solution so perfectly simple he was

amazed he had taken so long to getting around to it. One which would please and satisfy them both—but would also wipe the slate clean.

Because in a crazy way, he felt responsible for what had just happened. He would never have taken her so swiftly and perfunctorily if he had known she was an innocent. To be truthful, he would not have taken her at all. But he had and—while he had just shown her how pleasurable certain aspects of sex could be—she still had a lot to learn. And shouldn't he be the one to teach her? Might that not more than compensate for the fact that he had unwittingly taken her virginity?

Abruptly, he turned his back on her—went to look out over the sweeping grounds. He noticed that the lawns which swept down to the lake were ragged at the edges, and that the lake itself looked clogged with debris. Encroaching weeds had made a mockery of the flowerbeds and some had even disappeared completely.

Had he been crazy to come up with this scheme—to uproot his New York life and establish himself in a brand-new part of the world? Yet his father's death had unsettled him—made him aware of the impermanence of life and the need to chase your dreams.

Turning back to face her, he was aware that at least his arousal had subsided and was grateful for the fact that she had grabbed the coverlet and had slithered it over the enticement of her curves.

'I need to get showered and dressed,' he said shortly.

Hearing the abrupt note of dismissal in his voice, Cathy eyed her discarded uniform doubtfully, realising that she was going to have to leave here in a completely dishevelled state. What if she bumped into one of the other staff— how on earth would she be able to explain her appearance? 'I'll—'

'You can use the bathroom after me,' he said. With an effort, he flicked her a glance—barely able to look at her tousled golden beauty lest it make him break his resolve and go over there and ravish her. He smiled with predatory pleasure. 'And I want you to be ready at eight tonight,' he added softly.

Cathy's heart missed a beat; she thought she must be imagining things. Was he asking her out on a *date*? 'Tonight?'

'That's right. There's a party at the polo club—what they're calling a low-key celebration of my successful takeover—and you're coming with me.'

She stared at him incredulously. 'B-but, why? I mean, why me?'

His eyes narrowed. Was she really as disingenuous as she seemed? Didn't she realise that even a man of his calibre found her tight, lush body irresistible? Up until now those sinful curves had been woefully under-used—but not for much longer.

'These occasions are always easier if you have someone beside you to deflect some of the inevitable attention—and also, I intend taking you to bed afterwards,' he drawled, and his eyes glittered her a silent, sensual message. 'But neither of us should forget that you are completely untutored—and royal princes expect their mistresses to be skilful.'

Cathy's pulse rocketed as one word reverberated over and over again. *'Mistress?'* she gasped.

'I rather think what we've just been doing qualifies you for the role, don't you, Cathy?'

'I...I don't know what to say,' she breathed.

'Then say nothing. Women usually say far too much when they would be better remaining silent and simply looking beautiful.' He glittered her a look. 'And beauty is marred by too much make-up—so please don't wear quite so much in future because I can assure you that I don't find it attractive.'

'That was...that was Rupert's idea,' she blurted out.

'Oh, was it?' he questioned thoughtfully as he studied the too-sooty eyes and suddenly her tarty transformation began to make sense. What a creep the Englishman was! 'Well, from now on—you will take instruction only from me in the best way to present yourself as my mistress. You show great potential for the position, *cara mia*. I should never have taken your virginity— indeed, you are the only virgin I have ever bedded—and that cannot now be undone. But perhaps I can in some way redress the balance.'

Cathy stared at him, her heart pounding wildly, her mouth drying. 'What are you talking about?'

'Why, in return for having robbed you of your innocence, I intend teaching you everything I know about the art of love-making.' He gave a slow and provocative smile. 'And that way, we can call it quits.'

CHAPTER FIVE

THE violet shadows of evening were lengthening and the fading light seemed to pick out the brightness of the flowers which were packed so tightly into the small garden. Xaviero paused, his eyes narrowing as he took in the unexpected kaleidoscope of colour which appeared before him.

The path leading to Cathy's cottage was lined on either side by the purple haze of lavender and tall delphiniums which stood like cobalt arrows against the grey flint of the garden wall. Creamy-pink roses scrambled over a trellis—while blooms which looked like bells and others which resembled stars all jostled and billowed for space in the flowerbeds. And everywhere there were drifts of scent—some subtle, some powerful but all of them beguiling to his senses. It was a place of real beauty, and of calm.

For a moment he lingered there, his senses drinking in the extraordinary peace of the place as he realised that his expectations had been confounded. Hadn't he thought that the little chambermaid might live in some faceless and featureless little apartment in the nearby village? A humble abode whose very modesty would reinforce her subservience to him.

Yet this place was nothing like that.

At that moment the front door opened—she must have been watching him from inside—and there she stood, framed in the doorway and staring at him, as if she couldn't quite believe he was there. Truth to tell, he couldn't quite believe it himself.

But the fire Cathy had lit within him still burned. It had been burning all day, all during the dull, dry lawyers' meetings and his subsequent sessions with a local horse-breeder. He hadn't been able to get her out of his mind, remembering with painfully acute clarity just how good it had felt to thrust into that hot, virgin tightness of hers. Maybe he had underestimated the primeval pleasure that her innocence had given him.

Subduing the aching response to his thoughts, he raised his black eyebrows. 'Ready?'

Although she registered the fact that it wasn't the most affectionate of greetings, Cathy's smile was nonetheless wide and genuine—because hadn't she been dreading that he might have had second thoughts and changed his mind about taking her out? But no, he was here to take her to some fancy polo-club do and it hadn't been some kind of wild and crazy dream, after all. Prince Xaviero of Zaffirinthos really *had* taken her bed and then announced that she was to be a royal mistress and he was to instruct her in the things which pleased him!

Could she have said no?

She thought of his cold-blooded reasoning. *That way, we can call it quits.* In view of that, then *shouldn't* she have said no? But the truth of the matter was that her heart felt a bursting kind of happiness that he was here at all—and wasn't her body eager for more of his expert touch?

She looked up at him uncertainly, fingers fluttering over the black dress which skimmed her hips. 'Is this…okay? They say you can't go wrong with black but I wasn't sure if it would be suitable for a polo club? You see, well—I've…well, I've never actually been to one before.'

Golden eyes swept over her. The dress was unremarkable—a cheap creation which neither emphasised nor concealed her figure, while the glorious sun-ripe hair was tied back in some sort of ribbon. But at least she had heeded his words about not plastering her face with make up—the lightest touch of mascara and lipstick now emphasised her subtle beauty rather than parodying it.

'The dress is fine—although in future I may buy you dresses more pleasing to the eye. But there is one thing about your appearance which jars.' He walked towards her and, without warning, reached for the band which constrained her hair, slithering it off with an impatient jerk so that her hair tumbled wildly all over her shoulders. For a moment, he stared down into aquamarine eyes so wide and so deep that he felt as if he might drown in them. 'Don't ever wear your hair like that when you're with me,' he said unevenly. 'I like it loose. Understand?'

Cathy felt the tendrils falling around her face, acknowledging the dark mastery of his command even while a squeak of protest demanded to make itself heard. It was outrageous that he should come out with something as old-fashioned and bossy as that, she thought weakly. Prince he might be, but did he have the right to speak to her in that way?

'Understand?' he repeated.

Yet, dazed by his proximity and the sensual recall of his touch, all she could do was nod. 'Yes,' she whispered.

For a moment the sight of her wide eyes and trembling lips tempted him into ringing up the club and telling them he'd changed his mind. But something was stopping him and he wasn't sure what it was. Perhaps the faint air of insecurity about her which, infuriatingly, made him feel that he ought to spoil her. Take her out and give her a taste of the high life—as if in that way he could repay her for what he had already taken and would later take from her again.

His mouth hardened, because the last thing he wanted to feel was any kind of *conscience* about her. She had wanted him just as badly—and every woman had to lose her virginity *some* day. So why not lose it to the best? 'My car is parked at the end of the lane,' he said.

It felt odd to be walking down a dusty summer lane with the golden-eyed Prince and odder still to remember what had taken place between them. Cathy was conscious of the chauffeur's curious looks as he held the door open for her. Was he wondering what the Prince was playing at? Or maybe this was the kind of thing he did all the time and she was only one in a long series of women who had climbed so meekly into the back of the luxury limousine.

That thought sat uncomfortably with her and she waited for—and wanted—Xaviero to take her in his arms once they were enclosed within the tinted luxury of the car. To blot out all her misgivings with the power of his kiss. But he didn't. Instead, he simply leaned back against the soft leather seat, his long legs spread out in front of him while he surveyed her from between the narrowed golden eyes.

'Your house is not what I was…expecting,' he observed slowly.

It sounded more like a question than a compliment and Cathy knew exactly what he meant. 'On a chambermaid's salary, you mean?'

He shrugged. 'How the hell should I know? I have no idea what chambermaids earn.'

No, of course he wouldn't. Princes didn't draw salaries like ordinary folk, did they? What must it be like to exist inside a great, privileged bubble which separated you from the rest of the world? she wondered. 'My great-aunt left it to me. She brought me up when my parents died. It's…' Her words trailed off. Wasn't *he*, as the Prince, supposed to initiate all conversation— so maybe that meant just answering his questions and not bothering to elaborate on them. She clamped her lips shut.

'It's what?'

'You aren't really interested.'

He felt a mixture of amusement and irritation. 'Oh, aren't I?' he questioned silkily. 'One session of sex and already you can predict what I'm thinking? I know that all women like to think they're mind-readers—but that really must be breaking some kind of record.'

Cathy blushed. How *cynical*. How *hard-bitten*. What had he said? *One session of sex*. It was a hateful way to describe what had happened between them.

'The cottage is one of the reasons I stay round here—well, the garden mainly,' she said stiffly. 'I can't imagine ever finding anywhere else as beautiful. And…well, gardening's my hobby— though it always sounds so tame when someone my age admits that they like it.'

'Or elemental,' he amended surprisingly. 'Some people might consider it sexy to think of a woman bending over a flowerbed, with mud on her hands.'

'Really?' she questioned, not believing him.

'Yes, really.' Hearing the wooden quality of

her tone, Xaviero studied the way her little teeth were digging into the cushioned curve of her lower lip, and he smiled. 'You look disappointed,' he murmured. 'Are you wondering why I haven't yet kissed you?'

'Not at all,' she lied.

He laughed. 'Ah, but you must learn not to blush when you tell an untruth,' he murmured and saw her colour deepen even more.

'I wasn't—'

'Yes, you were. There should be few secrets between lovers. If you're wondering why I haven't yet kissed you, can't you think of a reason why that might be?'

Like the class dunce who had been unexpectedly picked out to answer a question by the teacher, Cathy was eager to please. 'Because you don't want your driver to see us?'

Xaviero clicked his tongue. How very mundane of her—but then what could he expect? She *was* a very ordinary woman. Impatiently, he shook his head. 'You think I would leave that to chance?' he mocked. 'The back of the car is completely soundproofed so the driver hears nothing. At the touch of a button, blinds will float down over all the windows, concealing us from the prying eyes of the outside world. Why, I could make love to you now and nobody but us would know.'

'Oh,' said Cathy, aware of an aching feeling of disappointment.

His impatience fled as he registered her un-ashamed frustration. 'Yes, I know. You want it and I want it, but it will be a rushed encounter—and what is more, we will both arrive at the club in a state of disarray which will not be particu-larly good for my reputation.'

And what about mine? Cathy wanted to ask. 'Oh, I see.'

'No, I don't think you do.' He reached over to take a silken lock of hair between thumb and forefinger and twisted it. 'The sexual appetite is like any other, Cathy—its needs are many and must be tempered accordingly. Sometimes—like what happened between us today—the hunger is fierce and urgent and must be instantly assuaged. And at other times, well—the anticipation of the feast to come sharpens the taste buds and heightens the pleasure.' His eyes gleamed. 'This evening may be tedious—as so many of these functions are—but rather than sinking into the torpor of that tedium, I shall instead allow my senses to tingle with the thought of just what I am going to do with you later.'

Cathy's mouth dried—partly with desire and partly with shock as she registered his arrogant statement. *Just what I am going to do with you later.* Why, he made her sound so malleable! 'That's if I let you,' she retorted.

Xaviero tensed and then gave a slow smile. 'Oh, you'll *let me*,' he vowed softly. 'Now come over here and kiss me, little chambermaid.'

'But I thought—'

'Mistresses aren't required to *think*—their talents are of a far more practical nature,' he amended silkily. 'So come over here. Now. And kiss me.'

For a moment Cathy sat there. His words made her feel more like a doll than a person and she suddenly realised that this man could easily hurt her. *So wouldn't it be sensible to get out now—*

before it was too late? She could feel his eyes on her—that distinctive golden gaze raking over her. He was sprawled back against the seat, eyeing her with lazy amusement as if sensing her inner struggle.

So did he feel triumph over the way she lost the battle she had half-heartedly been fighting? Leaning over him instead and eagerly pressing her lips to his—not caring about pride or conscience or reputation or getting hurt. Not caring about anything—other than the urgent need to find herself tightly in his arms once more.

She heard him give a little murmur of approval as he drew her against him, before she felt him take control—expertly coaxing her lips open and letting his tongue slide inside her mouth.

Cathy gasped as, in an instant, all those new feelings he had ignited earlier came flooding back in a thick, sweet wave and she clung to his broad shoulders as if she could never bear to let him go. Pressing her body closer, she heard his shuddered little groan and that felt like some kind of small victory.

But if it was Cathy who initiated the kiss, it was Xaviero who demonstrated his mastery by terminating it, gently prising her fingers from his shoulders and placing them firmly in her lap, leaving her breathless and aching as she stared up at him in mute disappointment.

'You must learn to control your appetite, my eager young pupil,' he chided softly, though he felt the wild thunder of his heart as he steadied his breath. 'There is a time and a place for greed, and that time is not now.'

In an effort to distract himself, Xaviero turned to glance out of the window as the car passed through wide gates and up a long gravelled drive. At its end stood an imposing brightly lit and colonnaded white house with a whole fleet of top-of-the-range cars and several chauffeurs standing in a little huddle beside them. He saw one of them glance up and spot the car approaching and it was as if they were all suddenly galvanised into action. Inside the illuminated building he could see figures beginning to hurry around and mentally he prepared to deliver the image of himself the public always expected.

'We're here,' he said, raking his fingers back through his hair. 'And they've seen us.'

Cathy glanced at the sudden cool mask which had replaced the dark passion on his face. 'You don't sound very…keen.'

He should have been irritated by her intrusive observation—but the appeal in her wide blue eyes meant that he was momentarily disarmed. Couldn't he relax his guard for once, just a little? This little chambermaid would never make the error of attaching any significance to any confidences he might share with her—and if she tried, he would merely point out her error so that she would not repeat it. 'I'd much rather be making love to you,' he admitted softly.

And that one murmured comment, along with the sizzling golden look which accompanied it, was enough to make Cathy feel as if she were walking on air as the car door was opened for them.

'And so would I,' she whispered shyly, but her momentary pleasure was eclipsed by nerves as she saw the glamorous women who were assembling to meet them. They were decked in glittering jewels, their skin faintly tanned, pampered and massaged—she felt anxiety flood through her. How could she possibly compete in her cheap little chain-store dress when they all looked like expensive birds of paradise?

Uncomfortably, Cathy followed Xaviero into the banqueting hall, where every table setting seemed to contain a whole canteen of cutlery— but at least she'd helped out at enough formal banquets at the hotel to know which was the correct knife and fork to use.

Picking at her meal, Cathy noticed that everyone waited until Xaviero had begun to eat before they, too, followed suit. How wearing that must get, she thought. She found herself seated in between two very wealthy landowners who wouldn't have given her a second glance if she'd been changing their duvet cover.

But Xaviero had, hadn't he?

Cathy swallowed. He might be arrogant, and proud. He might have taken her to bed and she might have foolishly let him—but nothing could detract from the fact that he had wanted her, just the way she was. And she had wanted him. In fact, if only he really *were* that man in denim and not a prince, then they wouldn't have to be sitting here, having to endure these stilted conversations. They could have been snuggled up under their own duvet—making love and maybe making some kind of future together.

'I'm sure I've seen you somewhere before, Cathy,' one of the landowners was saying to her.

Cathy felt her heart begin to pound with trepidation. 'I…I don't think so—'

'Good heavens—you're not…' The man pushed his scarlet face closer and frowned. 'You don't by any chance work at Rupert Sanderson's hotel, do you?'

Cathy froze and looked across the table in alarm—to find a pair of curious golden eyes fixed on her. Obviously Xaviero had heard every word and was watching her, waiting to hear what she would say.

For one tempting moment she thought about the reaction she'd get if she told the truth. That she was the chambermaid at the hotel he was currently buying and that she'd tugged Egyptian cotton sheets over the Prince's king-sized bed before letting him make love to her on it?

She realised that the landowner was still waiting for her answer and she looked into Xaviero's eyes as if seeking an answer there and, to her astonishment, he gave her a slow smile.

'Yes, Cathy works locally at the hotel—and has kindly agreed to be my guide while I'm here. Aren't I lucky?' he murmured, noticing that the redhead who had been flirting with him all evening was now flicking the little chambermaid a superior glance. Thoughtfully, his eyes narrowed, as he realised that he had not done Cathy justice. 'It helps that she's very beautiful, of course,' he added softly.

Cathy felt the rush of colour to her cheeks at the faint ripple of surprise this remark produced—before the chatter resumed around the table. And although she was pleased that Xaviero had come to her rescue, she wished he hadn't felt the need to tell a blatant lie like that.

Under his mocking stare she noticed the fractional dilation of his eyes. Saw the way the tip of his tongue had touched one corner of his lips as if deliberately reminding her of the sweet delight those same lips had brought to her earlier. And suddenly she didn't care if he'd lied about her being beautiful. When he looked at her like that, she actually *felt* beautiful. Just as she'd felt when he'd gazed down at her naked body as if he couldn't quite believe his eyes.

Was she alone in feeling the tension which fizzed across the table between them? Was he aware that every time his lips curved into a slow and speculative smile she experienced the warm pooling of desire at the pit of her stomach? The impatience to be alone with him and away with these people who fawned over every word he said. The women on either side of him might have been flirting outrageously—but *she* was the woman he had chosen to be his lover!

Her pulse skittered as he stood up and made a brief speech, telling the enthralled audience how delighted he was to have purchased such a prestigious club and his plans to create a world-class polo school there. But Cathy watched the faces of the other diners as they listened to him and laughed conspicuously loudly at his jokes. Rapt and rapacious—the women surveyed him with open hunger while the men regarded him with a kind of grudging envy. What a strange world this was, she thought. One where everyone wants something from him.

And don't you? taunted the voice of her conscience. *Don't you want most of all?*

No. She was modest by nature and modest in her expectations. All she wanted was to feel his arms around her again. To feel the warmth of his skin and the thunder of his heart against her heart. She felt her mouth drying as he finished his speech and looked straight into her eyes as the applause rang out through the vast room.

Needing the washroom, she rose to her feet and saw that Xaviero had mirrored her movement— which in turn caused the entire table to stand up! How awful, she thought. You could never just sneak out if you were a royal. In the restroom, she splashed some cold water over her heated cheeks, battled a brush through the thick hair, and when she emerged it was to find Xaviero standing by the entrance to the ballroom. It took a moment or two before she registered that he was waiting for *her*.

In that moment she felt nervous and slightly out of her depth—but she had to say *something*. 'Thank you for coming to my rescue back there,' she said quietly.

He shrugged and gave a dismissive wave of his hand. 'No thanks are required. The man was nothing but a crashing snob and I'm sorry you had to be subjected to him.'

Cathy glowed with pleasure at his kindness, wanting to compliment him—just as he had complimented her. 'And I...I really liked your speech,' she ventured softly.

It was the most straightforward thing anyone had said to him in a long time and she sounded as if she really meant it. For a moment Xaviero looked down into her upturned face, thinking how simple her life must be. How unlike those glittering and bejewelled women with their bony shoulders who had vied shamelessly for his attention all evening. And suddenly, the memory of her smile the first time she'd seen him stirred in him a distant memory. Sunny and uncomplicated and full of innocent promise.

'Come on, we're leaving,' he said suddenly.

She glanced down the corridor into the still-packed ballroom and thought about their two glaringly empty chairs. 'But won't…won't people mind?'

'Mind? I don't care if they do,' he murmured, meeting her wide-eyed question with a smile. 'It is time for your next lesson, my beauty. It's going to be a very long and extensive lesson—and I, for one, can't wait for it to begin.'

CHAPTER SIX

'GOING out somewhere tonight, are you, Cathy?' Momentarily, Cathy froze in the act of picking up her handbag as Rupert's words stopped her in her tracks. Composing her face, she turned around, preparing to face him—remembering what Xaviero had told her when she'd worried aloud about people finding out that they were lovers.

'So what? You have nothing to hide, *cara*,' he had murmured casually. 'And neither do I. Every man is entitled to a mistress.'

It had made her briefly wonder why he had used the term 'mistress' instead of 'girlfriend', when he wasn't even married. But maybe that was what princes did when they acquired a lover who was also a commoner. They erected boundaries—so that the lover wouldn't ever make the mistake of thinking that there might be some kind of future in their affair.

Trying to hide her nerves, she gave a slightly wobbly smile because Rupert was still standing in front of her, blocking her way and clearly expecting some kind of answer to his question.

'Actually, I'm staying home tonight,' she said, noticing her boss's eyes straying to the bulging carrier bags at her feet. She'd rushed down to the village at lunchtime and had bought crusty wholemeal bread and some thick slices of ham from the butcher.

'Cooking dinner for lover-boy, are we?' he sneered.

Cathy swallowed and then drew her shoulders back. If Xaviero liked her enough to want to spend time with her, then there was no way she was going to let Rupert Sanderson look down his nose at her! 'No, we're having salad tonight,' she answered calmly.

Rupert looked irritated. 'He could have a silver-service dinner any night of the week right here and yet he seems to prefer slumming it with you! And we all know why that is, don't we?' His petulant voice lowered to a kind of hiss. 'But better not get *too* used to it. You may have managed to entice a prince into your bed, Cathy—but he'll drop you like a hot potato once the novelty has worn off.'

Cathy froze—because wasn't her boss only articulating thoughts she'd had a hundred times herself since she'd become Xaviero's lover? Heart pounding, she lifted up her chin and looked him directly in the eye. 'May I please pass?' she questioned politely.

'Feel free.' He fixed his gaze on her breasts. 'Nice blouse, Cathy—is it new?'

As she passed by Cathy blushed—because yes, it *was* a nice blouse. In fact, it was an extremely beautiful blouse—made out of the softest silk chiffon imaginable, and covered in lots of tiny little flowers so that it resembled a summer meadow. And Xaviero had bought it for her.

It had arrived in a fancy box, which she'd had to collect from the village post office. Cathy had no experience of costly clothes, but even with her untutored eye she immediately sensed that the blouse was worth a small fortune. It transformed an old pair of jeans into an eye-catching outfit and had made Xaviero's eyes narrow with appreciation.

Next, a large box of fine French lingerie had been delivered—and the Prince had waved her protests aside with a careless gesture of his hand. He didn't care that she was reluctant to accept gifts from him, he told her—*he wanted to give them to her, and his wishes were paramount.*

'I don't want you in cheap underwear,' he had murmured as he'd slowly peeled off a pair of sheer lace cami-knickers and watched her squirm with delight. 'My mistress must be clothed in silk and satin.'

It had made her feel rather odd. A bit like an object. But then his expert lips and seeking fingers would get to work and dissolve any lingering doubts—replacing them with a sense of wonder that he should desire her as much as he did.

As she walked down the flower-banked path to her cottage Cathy reflected that her weeks with the Prince had been everything that any woman could ever have wished for.

Well, maybe *some* women might have objected to the fact that they didn't go out very much—though he had certainly offered to take her. The trouble was that going out with a prince was beset with difficulties. A supposedly incognito visit to the cinema had been spoiled when word had got out that a European royal was present. Maybe it had been the attendance of his body-guards who had given the game away, no matter how discreet they had tried to be. And conse-quently, the staff had made a fawning kind of fuss of him.

Cathy had noticed how much he hated being recognised; she hated it, too—and not just because she was thrust aside into the shadows. Understandably Xaviero was much more uptight when he was being observed by other people. So she had suggested that they stay at home, in her little cottage. They could eat supper outside if the weather was fine—in the seclusion of the small garden. And if it rained, then they could watch

DVDs while cuddled up on the sofa, just like any other couple.

To her surprise, he had agreed—and to her even greater surprise, he hadn't grown bored with the arrangement. On the contrary, Xaviero seemed to love the simple life, which was all she could offer him. And it gave Cathy almost as much pleasure as his love-making—to see her prince relax in the relative anonymity of her little home.

He's not your *prince*, she reminded herself fiercely as she dumped the two carrier bags on the kitchen table and went out into the garden to pull some potatoes from the ground.

She was so busy tugging at the tiny little vegetables that she didn't hear anyone come into the garden. In fact, the first she knew that Xaviero was present was the touch of his hands at her waist. Such an innocent touch and yet it had the power to make her feel weak with wanting.

'Xaviero,' she breathed.

'You were expecting someone else?' came his wry reply as he turned her round to face him.

'I'm all muddy!'

He stared down into her flushed and healthy-looking cheeks—at the bright aquamarine eyes which sparkled like blue stars. She was...enchanting. Completely without guile or affectation. 'Who cares?' he murmured as he lowered his head to kiss her.

The kiss became breathless—and the potatoes scattered around their feet. Inside, she quickly washed the mud from her hands and then her lover carried her to bed, where they made love with an urgent kind of fervour which suggested that they might have been apart for weeks, rather than mere hours.

And afterwards he pulled her up to lie against his warm body, kissing the top of her head and breathing in the silky scent of her hair.

'That was...*amazing*,' he murmured, his fingers settling over one soft breast. 'Who taught you to do that?'

'You did,' she whispered. Just as he had taught her everything. Tightening her arms around him, Cathy felt the powerful body relax against hers and wished that the world outside this cottage didn't exist. That they could stay marooned in here in a world of make-believe, where she could pretend that he was simply Xaviero—the man whose golden-eyed beauty had grown to dominate her world.

He began to drift off to sleep beside her and she could hear nothing but the steadying of his breathing, and the ticking of her bedside clock. Oh, how she hated that little clock which ruthlessly whittled away the minutes they spent with each other. Hands which crept round so agonisingly slowly when Xaviero was absent that they seemed almost stationary. But when he was here…well, that was when time would play cruel tricks—greedily running away with itself until the alarm on his cell phone reminded him that it was time to leave.

Then, in the early hours he would prise himself from her warm embrace, pulling on his clothes to slip out into the balmy summer air where his chauffeur was waiting patiently at the end of the lane, ready to drive him the short distance to the hotel.

'Why don't you…stay?' she had ventured, on

that blissful first night in his arms—when she had lain there dazed in the sweet aftermath of his love-making.

'I can never stay the night with you, Cathy,' he had stated, his voice suddenly hard and resolute.

Too full of emotion and pleasure to heed the unmistakable caution which smouldered at the depths of his golden eyes, she had looked up into his face with innocent bewilderment. 'Why not?'

'Because staying a whole night is a statement. It implies a commitment which is not present— and to do so will compromise both of us.' He had lifted her chin then. Stared hard into her eyes. 'And you know that this is nothing but a very temporary affair, don't you—because I made that clear from the beginning?'

'Yes. Yes, of course I do,' she'd said, trying to keep her voice from trembling. Telling herself that at least he wasn't lying to her—or keeping false hopes alive by pretending that there might be some kind of future in it. Because she had known from the outset that there wasn't. Far better to simply revel in every glorious and unbelievable moment than try to hang onto a hopeless dream.

Beside her, Xaviero stirred from his brief sleep. 'Cathy?'

She rolled over to face him, their gazes meeting in the confined space of her bed, and her heart turned over with longing. 'What?'

'This.' He slid her hand between his thighs until her fingers collided with his hotly aroused flesh and Cathy's lips parted.

'Again?' she whispered breathlessly.

'*Sì*, again,' he agreed unsteadily.

She swallowed as the familiar heat of desire began to unfurl in her stomach. 'So…soon?' she managed huskily.

'Always. Always! Because you drive me crazy!' he said fiercely. 'Crazier than any woman I have ever bedded!'

Feeling his hands encircle her waist, Cathy drifted her lips to his neck and trailed her mouth lightly over his silken flesh. 'Do I?'

'*Oddio*, I think I have taught you a little too well,' he said unsteadily as he lifted her up and then brought her slowly down on top of him and she gasped as she felt him fill her.

She didn't have the time or the inclination to question him—not then, when he was moving her up and down on his swollen shaft like that. Taking her to that sweet place of release where the rest of the world and all its nagging doubts could be forgotten. When she could cry out his name with uninhibited joy and he would think it was simply the orgasm speaking and not a shout of fervour from her heart.

Much later, they clambered back into their clothes and Cathy concocted a meal, while Xaviero opened some of the wine he'd brought with him. Tipping the ruby liquid into the chunky little tumblers she kept in her kitchen, he smiled.

'One of the finest wines in the world,' he murmured. 'And here we are drinking it from tooth-mugs!'

Cathy put a little bowl of cherry tomatoes on the table and turned to look at him. 'You want me to get some proper wine glasses?'

He looked at her, and at that moment Xaviero

felt a sharp longing for a world he would never really know—where every purchase had to be calculated and assessed. Where things were bought for necessity and governed by cost—without bringing elegance or beauty into the equation. He would no more have drunk from glasses like this in his own home than he would have lapped wine from a saucer—but for now they seemed to symbolise a sense of simplicity he had never known.

'I don't want you to change anything,' he said.

Cathy bit her lip as she went back inside the cottage to get the butter dish—afraid that her sudden fears would show on her face, and scare him. The very real fear of how on earth she was going to cope with life once Xaviero had left it.

But doubts could grow in your mind—even if you didn't want them to—and Cathy barely touched her meal, though she drank deeply of the rich Italian wine. Xaviero had shared her life these past weeks and yet she realised that she knew very little about him. Or at least about his other life. His royal life.

'Tell me about Zaffirinthos,' she said suddenly.

'Not now, Cathy.' He yawned.

'Yes, now,' she said stubbornly. 'Why not?'

His lips curved into a reluctant smile as he watched her push a stray strand of thick blonde hair from her flushed cheek, recognising that she was a beguiling mixture of innocence and outspokenness. She was a complete *natural*, he realised—and it was still enough of a novelty not to irritate him. And yet wasn't one of her most appealing qualities the fact that she was so biddable—so willing to be taught? Why, if he'd told her that it increased his sexual pleasure to have her dance naked around him beforehand, she would have gone about it in an instant!

His smile was one of rare indulgence. 'And what—specifically—do you want to know about Zaffirinthos?'

'Everything,' she answered, wondering if she had imagined that faintly patronising tone.

'But surely you must already know something? Some facts you picked up on the Internet. Because I can't believe you didn't look me up when you discovered who I was,' he drawled. 'People always do.'

Cathy found herself colouring, like a child who had been caught with her fingers in the cookie jar. Or some stupid little royal groupie. 'Obviously I found out some things—'

'Of course you did.' His smile was faintly cynical. 'What things?'

'Not the kind of things I'd really like to know.'

'And what might they be?'

'Oh, I don't know.' She screwed the lid back on the mayonnaise. 'Like what kind of child-hood you had?'

If anyone else had dared quiz him about something so personal, he would have dismissed it as an outrageous imposition—but Cathy had a soft way of asking which was hard to resist. 'It was a child-hood in two halves,' he said thoughtfully. 'The first bit was idyllic—and then my mother died.'

Her heart went out to him—because didn't she know only too well the pain of *that*? 'And every-thing changed?' she prompted quietly.

'Totally. My father was utterly bereft.' He

stared at the ceiling. The depth of his father's grief had taught him the dangers of emotional dependence as well as the temporary nature of happiness. 'And then he turned all his attention into grooming my older brother to succeed him, as King. It meant a lot of freedom for me—so I was able to concentrate on my riding. That's when I first started to learn about polo.'

Cathy experienced another wrench of sympathy—because too much freedom for a child could sometimes mean loneliness. She tried to imagine Xaviero as a little boy, doubly bereaved in a way—first by his mother's death and then by his father's withdrawal. And while she knew all about bereavement, at least she had enjoyed a close relationship with her great-aunt. 'And your brother is now King,' she said.

'That's right. My father died last year and big brother is now in charge,' said Xaviero, a sudden edge to his voice. 'Busy modernising Zaffirinthos with his sweeping reforms.'

But Cathy wasn't interested in sweeping reforms—she wanted to see the island through her lover's eyes. 'And is it very beautiful?' she asked. 'Zaffirinthos?'

'Very beautiful,' he murmured. But somehow her questions made him realise how long he'd been away—and reinforced his sense of exile. He had not returned since his brother's coronation, for reasons which were essentially primitive and guilt-inducing. Boyhood rivalries ran deep as blood itself, he thought grimly—and hadn't there been a part of him which had always resented the accident of birth which had ensured that Casimiro would inherit the crown? Power was easy to come by, and Xaviero had built up his own power-base through his own hard work—but no one could deny the lure of ruling a country…

He realised that Cathy was still looking at him, her aquamarine eyes searching his face as she waited for him to paint the perfect, holiday-brochure picture of his paradise home.

He shrugged his shoulders. Well, he would give her the brochure version. Why not? He would be her fantasy prince in his fantasy land and that could be the memory she would keep of him. 'It has forests so green that, like Ireland, it is known as the emerald isle. And the best beaches in the world, with sand as pale as sugar. And we have a bay with the bluest water—even bluer than your eyes, *cara*—where the rare caretta-caretta turtles come to lay their eggs on summer nights so still that you can almost hear the stars shooting across the sky.'

Cathy looked at him and couldn't suppress a little sigh of longing. His lyrical words painted pictures, yes—but also helped create an image of the man she wanted him to be. One who was romantic, and caring. Would it be too much to hope that he cared a little bit about her? Hadn't he just compared her eyes to the bluest sea and then called her 'darling' in Italian? How easy it would be to read too much into a simple remark like that—perhaps imagining that he wanted more from her than just being his willing bed-partner. 'It sounds…it sounds like paradise,' she said wistfully.

'Oh, it is,' he agreed evenly, because he knew exactly what she was doing. She wanted him to say that he would take her there. Was she building little fantasies about visiting the magnificent palace, perhaps—mistakenly imagining that she might have some place there? In which case, she should be very careful not to confuse fantasy with reality.

'But you know, of course, that I can never take you there,' he said softly, and, reaching out, he pulled her down onto his lap.

On one level, of course she had known that—but on another, she had hoped… Cathy bit her lip. She had hoped for what every woman in her situation would hope for—no matter how foolish that hope. And why had he made that completely unnecessary statement, which necessitated her asking a question she didn't really want to ask? Suddenly, she found herself on the defensive.

'Why not?'

He lifted her chin with the tip of his finger. 'Because my people would never accept me openly flaunting a lover there. They are less accepting of modern sexual manners than you are here.'

'They would look down on me, I suppose?' she questioned shakily.

'Cathy,' he appealed. 'Don't do this.'

'Because, of course, it's always the woman who takes the blame, isn't it? They would never dare to think that their darling Prince might have something to do with it.'

'That,' he said warningly, 'is enough.'

Her lips were trembling. 'All right, it's enough. And actually, I'm pretty bored with the subject myself!'

'Well, you're the one who brought it up.'

'And you're the one who spoilt it.'

'Are you aware,' he questioned silkily, 'that if you spoke to me in such a way in the presence of others you could be accused of gross insubordination?'

Pull yourself together, Cathy told herself fiercely, banishing her foolish longings and pressing her lips hungrily to the base of his throat instead. 'You could—but only if I were your subject,' she objected as she inhaled his raw, masculine scent. 'Which, of course, I'm not.'

As he laughed Xaviero felt his irritation

dissolve, acknowledging that her native intelligence was surprising. And in a curious way she could have almost held her own when compared with other women he had bedded—all of them more high-born than her.

He had slept with heiresses whose own fortune could almost have matched his and he had slept with supermodels whose rangy bodies and exquisite features had graced countless glossy magazines.

Once, he had even dated an Oscar-winning English actress and had watched from his hotel suite while she had tearfully—and rather embarrassingly—accepted the award and dedicated it to *'the only man I have ever loved. The other man with the golden eyes.'* The press had gone crazy when they had worked out just who she was referring to. Later that night, they had made love beneath the metallic gaze of the statuette and a week later he had told her it was over— that public declarations of love had never been on the agenda.

But, out of all those confident and accomplished women, none had spoken to him with quite the same sunny simplicity as Cathy. It perplexed him—and he was not a man who did perplexity. Was it because her whole life had been spent in service that she seemed totally without guile or expectation? Or was it because she had been a virgin, and he had taken her innocence that she was so eager to be moulded by him?

He could see her looking at him questioningly, and he stroked at her silken hair. 'Who'd have thought,' he murmured, 'that a couple of weeks of intensive sexual tuition could make a humble little chambermaid such a perfect partner in bed?'

Cathy's smile didn't slip. She told herself not to react. That he probably wasn't *intending* to insult her. To concentrate instead on the way he made her feel when his fingers were stroking sweet enchantment over her skin. Anyway, perhaps he couldn't help it—maybe that arrogance was inbuilt and part of his unique royal make-up. Maybe princes from Zaffirinthos were *expected* to be arrogant. Far better to accept him for who he was and not try to change him. Why spoil what was never intended to be anything other than a brief, beautiful liaison? 'Who'd have thought it?' she agreed.

'So how do you do it?' he persisted.

'Oh, Xaviero—'

'No, I'm interested. It's more than a learning of sexual technique—though you are a surprisingly fast learner and a very satisfactory pupil. What's your secret, Cathy? Did you back up your practical skills with a little theory? Maybe you quietly read up one of those self-help books which advise women on the most effective way to deal with a powerful man?'

Leaning on her elbow, she looked at him. His arrogance was breathtaking—but sometimes even *he* overstepped the mark. Yet what could she say? Wouldn't he laugh in her face if she told him that her 'secret'—if that was what you could call it—was that she had schooled herself to *forget* that he was a prince? That at least in his arms she could pretend that he was the uncomplicated flirty man in denim she'd been so powerfully attracted to—the man with the golden eyes. And maybe he would take it the wrong way—because he *wasn't* that man, was he? Not really.

'Actually, no—I haven't. Those books aren't really directed at chambermaids,' she answered, deadpan.

'No. I don't suppose they are.' He surveyed her thoughtfully, and realised he couldn't keep putting off the inevitable. 'You know, I've been thinking…do you want me to help you find some other kind of job? Something different to do when…'

Cathy stilled as his words trailed off, the unusual hesitation alerting her to trouble. 'When…*what*, Xaviero?'

His eyes narrowed as he watched her, sizing up her reaction and preparing for tears, maybe hysteria. 'When all this is over.'

The silence grew like a gathering storm cloud while Cathy tried to dampen down the terrible feeling of fear which was clutching at her heart. Telling herself that she had known this was coming. It was just she hadn't been expecting it. Not now. Not yet.

'And…and is it all over?' she managed at last.

Xaviero relaxed a little. No tears. That was good. 'Not yet. But soon,' he murmured as he kissed the curving line of her jaw. 'Probably sooner than I thought.'

'Oh.'

'You've known all along that I've been planning to go to South America for the winter to look at horses?'

'Yes, of course,' answered Cathy, marvelling at the way she could make her voice sound so bright when inside her heart felt as if it were breaking in two.

'Well, a stallion I've had my eye on may be coming onto the market and it makes sense to go out there to look at it within the next few days. I complete on the hotel next week and I've been meeting with architects. The whole building is going to be remodelled to my specifications while I'm away—and I'm planning to keep on any existing staff who may wish to stay once it reverts into being a private house again.' He looked into her wary blue eyes.

'I'm just not sure how appropriate that might be, in your case.'

In the pause which followed, Cathy felt as if someone had taken a jagged shard of glass and speared it hard through her heart. She felt faint, dizzy, as his words had sent a chill of fear icing down her spine. 'I'm not sure I understand what you mean,' she said slowly.

Xaviero sighed. He had hoped that she might make this easy for him—without him actually having to spell out the gulf of inequality which would make any further liaison impossible. 'You know we can't continue being lovers when I return,' he said softly. 'I'll be building a settled life here, and it won't look good—not for either of us.'

'But especially not for you?'

He saw the hurt in her eyes which she was doing her best to disguise, but he knew he had to be honest with her. With a sudden sharp pang, he remembered how the doctors and even his own father had prevaricated when he had asked them whether his mother would live. They had given him hope. Stupid, misplaced hope. So that

Xaviero had learnt there was only one solution to misplaced hope—and that was to kill it.

'No,' he agreed heavily. 'You may find it uncomfortable if you stay here, Cathy. One of these days I may get around to looking around for a suitable partner,' he said, and then added, just so that there could be no possible misunderstanding, 'A bride. Because sooner or later I'm going to have to think about settling down.' He felt her stiffen. 'And I'm not sure how easy you might find that, either. If you were still employed here in some kind of chambermaid capacity, and I was bringing a woman back here and—'

'Asking me to change your dirty sheets?' she questioned bluntly.

'Cathy!'

'Well, it's true, isn't it?' Because he had sketched out the possible scenario and now wasn't it up to her to colour in the blanks? To imagine the whole ghastly reality of what he was saying to her. And that way, surely, there would be no space left for illusion or any more hurt? 'And, yes, you're right,

Xaviero. It really would be very awkward for both of you if I were still around.'

'Well, there isn't any *both*, is there? At least, not yet there isn't.' He traced the trembling line of her lips with a questing fingertip but she did not clamp her little white teeth around it and suck on it, as usually she would have done. 'Though I don't want you to feel you *have* to leave, just because of me.'

She stared at him, his royal status now forgotten—because in the circumstances it was irrelevant. This was her life, she realised—a life so very different from his. And it was where their two lives had merged and were now about to divide again, propelling her towards a scary and unknown future. 'Oh, of course I have to leave, Xaviero. There's no other alternative.' Or did he imagine that she would hover in the background of his life—some pale-faced little ghost of a woman he'd once known, while he made a new life and a family with his suitable bride?

Desperately, she tried to scrabble back a little dignity. 'But please don't feel bad about it, when we both know it's inevitable—we've known that all along. It's probably just the kick-start I needed. I've been telling myself I've been in a rut for ages and kept meaning to change—I just never got around to it before.'

His eyes narrowed as they studied her. 'If you want—I could perhaps help.' He saw the confusion in her face. 'You know—set you up in something, somewhere else.'

She recoiled. 'You mean…like…*pay me off*? What's that for—services rendered?'

'That isn't what I meant at all!' he snapped.

'Well, that's what it sounded like!'

For a moment he was tempted to leave her right then, to storm out of her little cottage and its surprisingly beautiful garden. A place where he had been able to shrug off privilege and position with his biddable little virgin whom he'd transformed into a near-perfect lover. And another man would one day benefit from all his tuition, he thought—with a sudden and unexpected spear of jealousy.

'Cathy, don't let's fight—not now,' he said, in

as placating a tone as he had ever used, pulling her face towards his.

And to Cathy's everlasting shame, she let him begin to kiss her. Even after all the things he had said to her, she just let him. All those stark statements he'd made which had hammered home her rightful place in the Prince's life. Which was nowhere. What woman with a shred of pride could sink back and revel in his expert caresses like this? But she wanted one more taste of him. One more erotic coupling with a man she recognised would never be equalled—not in anyone's life, but certainly not in hers.

He lifted his head and looked down into her wide aquamarine eyes and saw in them the telltale glimmer of tears. But for once he accepted the unnecessary intrusion of emotion—knowing that his biddable little pupil was about to learn that saying goodbye was the hardest lesson of all.

CHAPTER SEVEN

WITHOUT Xaviero, life suddenly felt lonely and scary—but Cathy did what all the advice columns suggested as a way of trying to forget him. Instead of sitting around and moping, she changed her life completely—deciding to grab every opportunity which came her way instead of just sitting back and going with the flow. Her Prince had gone, yes—but she had known from the beginning that he would. He had gone and he wasn't ever coming back and so she had better start learning to live with that and hope that this gnawing pain in her heart would some day lessen.

The first step in her recovery was leaving Colbridge—though really she didn't have much choice. Hadn't Xaviero himself spelt out in cruel and accurate detail just how difficult it would be if she were still there when he returned from South America?

Saying goodbye to friends and colleagues was harder than she'd thought, though it was no hardship leaving an openly curious Rupert, who had spent some of his profit on a red Lamborghini and was planning to open up another hotel in the south of France.

This time he *did* come right out and ask her if she'd been sleeping with the Prince, but although Cathy blushed she remained tight-lipped and told him it was really none of his business.

'I think your response speaks for itself,' he drawled.

'You can think what you like, Rupert.' Her cool reply clearly startled him—but, while Xaviero might have taught her about the pain of love, there was no doubt that sleeping with a prince had given her confidence.

It was harder to leave her little cottage where she'd lived for much of her life, and harder still to walk away from the garden on which she had fostered so much love and attention. But she rented it out to a plant-lover who promised to look after it, and moved to London, where she got a job in a famous bookshop situated right on Piccadilly, just along the road from Green Park. In a big, noisy capital city a bookshop seemed a warm and friendly place to be, and when they discovered her passion for plants and flowers she was quickly assigned to the Gardening, Cookery and Sport section of the store.

With the money she made from letting out her home she was able to rent a modest little studio flat just down the road from the bookshop. It was small, the heating was haphazard and it took a hundred and eight rickety steps just to reach it—but once you did, the view over the city was worth…

Worth what? mocked a voice in her head. A prince's ransom?

Heart racing, Cathy tried to shift the taunting thoughts her mind seemed determined to hang onto—but it was far from easy. She *missed* Xaviero. Really missed him. This felt like a broken heart. Like the real thing—while her break-up with Peter had been forgotten in a couple of days. This felt uncomfortably like love—even though she tried to tell herself again and again that she couldn't possibly have been in love with the golden-eyed Prince. It had just been a wonderful sexual awakening, she reasoned—and all she was doing was seeking to put a respectable label on the way she'd behaved.

And Cathy soon realised that being the spurned lover of a prince was a hopeless situation to be in. People always said there was no point in bottling things up—but she had little alternative. She couldn't *tell* anyone what had happened; quite apart from anything else—who in their right minds would ever believe her? Maybe the healing hands of time would help the vivid memories fade. And even though she enthusiastically threw herself into her new life, each night she cried softly into her pillow for the man who had captured her heart and her body so profoundly.

Autumn was approaching and she took to walking round Green Park in her lunch-hour and watching as the leaves began to turn golden brown and scrunched beneath her feet. And she drank her morning coffee in the dark staffroom at the very top of the building, and tried to make friends with the rest of the staff. There were all kinds of people working there, because book-shops seemed to attract a strange mixture. Lots of them were would-be writers, but there was also an ex-soldier, a hand model and a man who had once trained in Paris as a clown. And a part-time girl called Sandy who painted portraits of cats, which then went on to grace the covers of greetings cards.

It was Sandy who was beside her on the day Cathy turned on the Internet, and—when she thought nobody was looking—typed 'ZAFFIRINTHOS' into the search engine the way she did every morning. And Sandy who gripped her by the elbow as the world swam hor-rifically before Cathy's eyes and the large London bookshop became a blur.

'Cathy? For heaven's sake—what's the matter?' Sandy demanded. 'Cathy, are you *all right*?'

But Cathy barely heard the voice, which

seemed to come from a hundred miles away; she was too busy waiting for the dizziness to clear from her eyes and she uttered a small, disbelieving whimper as she took in the words which leapt out at her.

'Young royal fights for life: Zaffirinthos waits.'

'No!' she whimpered, shoving her fist into her mouth and feeling her knees begin to sway.

'Sit down!' urged Sandy.

Her head was placed between her knees and water was fetched for her to drink—and when the colour returned to her cheeks the section manager insisted that she go home for the rest of the day. She wanted to read the rest of the article but she could hardly start browsing the Internet in the store if they thought she was sick. Better get outside and buy a paper, or go to an Internet café or *something*.

'Are you pregnant?' muttered Sandy.

Cathy flinched at the unwitting hurtfulness of the remark. Actually, no, she wasn't—and hadn't *that* discovery proved unbearably poignant? For hadn't there been some crazy little part of her heart which had longed to hold onto some precious part of him, and to feel his child growing inside her belly? A hope banished when she'd stood in her tiny bathroom looking at a trembling stick which had stubbornly refused to turn blue.

'No, I'm not pregnant,' she said flatly.

Outside, the autumn wind was blustering in a cold funnel along the street, turning the newspaper she bought into a wild, flapping creature. She took it into a little café and ordered a cappuccino and then raked her way through the windblown pages. Zaffirinthos was a relatively small principality which was rarely newsworthy, but a young prince hovering between life and death would always make the international pages.

Her teeth chattering, she read:

King Casimiro of Zaffirinthos was today fighting for his life following a violent fall from his horse.

Cathy began to shake as the first thought which washed over her in a wave of intense relief was that...it wasn't Xaviero. But this was quickly followed by a second—a lurch of terrible guilt and sorrow—to realise that his brother should be lying stricken.

Poor Casimiro. Poor, poor Casimiro, she thought painfully as she read on.

The dashing royal, 34, who recently acceded to the throne of the tiny island kingdom, has been airlifted to the capital's hospital, where he remains in a coma. Doctors are refusing to comment on claims that the King is near death. His younger brother, Xaviero, 33 (pictured, right), is tonight on his way from South America to be at his stricken brother's bedside. This is not the first time that tragedy has struck the fabulously wealthy di Cesere family. In a cruel twist of fate, Queen Sophia—the King's mother and a noted beauty—died of a brain haemorrhage a quarter of a century ago.

Instinctively, Cathy began to examine the snatched photo, taken at Bogotá airport. Xaviero looked grim-faced and ravaged—his hand raised as if to strike the camera from the hands of the person taking the photograph. He looked *haunted*, she thought—and her heart went out to him.

Staring blandly at her now-cold coffee, she wondered if there was any way she could help. But Xaviero would be home by now, surrounded by advisors and guided by protocol, no doubt— what on earth could *she* possibly do?

Until she remembered that he had given her his cell-phone number—though possibly it was the only time a number had been handed out with the instruction *not* to use it.

'Only if it is absolutely necessary,' he had told her, his stern face leaving her in no doubt that he meant every word. 'If, for example, you were to discover that you were pregnant.' He had ac- knowledged her shocked little intake of breath, and had nodded, his face grim. 'And yes, I know we have taken every precaution, but accidents can and do happen—though, obviously, we both sincerely hope that this is not the case.'

Cathy bit her lip. What would she do if it were

anyone else? If it were a friend or a colleague, someone she cared about or even someone she *had* cared about? Why, even if it were Peter—her errant fiancé—she would send him a message straight away, telling him to hang on in there and that she was thinking of him. But this was different. Imagine the amount of people who would be trying to get in touch with a man as important as Xaviero. She was crazy to even think of trying.

As the days dragged by she couldn't settle. She kept thinking about Xaviero and wondering how his brother was faring—but even though she scoured the newspapers and the Internet for news there was no new update on his condition.

But one evening her conscience got the better of her and she knew she had to contact him. Who cared if it was the wrong thing to do, or if it was some diplomatic no-no? Or even if he thought her a fool for doing so? This wasn't about *her*—it was about *him*.

Sitting down on the rather scruffy sofa, she carefully composed words of comfort in her head before she dared translate them into a text message—terrified that he might think she was writing to him simply because she had an ulterior motive. In the end, she simply wrote: 'DESPERATELY SORRY TO HEAR YOUR BROTHER SO SICK. MY THOUGHTS WITH YOU. CATHY.' She hesitated before adding a single 'X', and then she pressed the 'send' button before she could change her mind.

She didn't expect to hear anything and when the phone began to ring a bit later on she thought it was probably Sandy, who'd been trying to persuade her to go to a comedy stand-up evening in town. But a quick glance at the screen of her cell phone set her heart racing in disbelief. It said…it said…

Xaviero?

Heart pounding, Cathy snatched up the receiver. 'H-hello?'

'Cathy?'

'Yes, it's me. Oh, Xaviero, I'm so s—'

His words cut across hers. 'Are you alone?'

'Yes. Yes, I am. Xaviero—how's your bro—?'

Again he interrupted. 'I can't talk for long and

I can't guarantee the security of the line. I need you to listen carefully, Cathy—and then to answer me. Can you come out to Zaffirinthos?'

'Wh-when?'

'Tomorrow.'

'*Tomorrow?* But, Xaviero—I don't under-stand—'

'I told you.' His voice sounded strained. 'I can't talk now—all I need is your answer—a simple yes, or no?'

Her mind was spinning as she tried to take in his extraordinary request, but on another level she registered the harshness of his tone. Her ac-quaintanceship with Xaviero might not have been long but it had certainly been intense and she knew that a tone like that brooked no argument.

Which meant that if she went, she would be going into the unknown…

'You hesitate, Cathy,' came the cool interrup-tion to her swirling thoughts.

His words brought Cathy snapping straight back into reality. Why on earth was she hesitat-ing for more than a second? This was the man who had haunted her dreams and her waking hours. The man who had made her feel like a woman for the first time in her life. Who had made her realise what glorious highs there could be in life…and what crashing lows, too. But he had taught her how to feel *alive*.

Yes, he was a prince, but in a way that was irrelevant—for the man with golden eyes had a power which he had exerted over her from the very start. Did he *need* her and wouldn't that be the most glorious thing in the world—to be needed by Xaviero? Cathy swallowed. He wasn't telling her anything and if she went to Zaffirinthos it would be on blind faith alone—a faith which might easily be misplaced and leave her as empty as a waterless well.

But there was no choice. Not when you felt the way she felt about Xaviero—no matter how many times she'd tried to tell herself that it was a complete waste of time. Sometimes you just had to follow your heart—to take a risk and leap into the unknown.

'Yes, I'll come to Zaffirinthos,' she said.

Standing in the ornate splendour of one of the palace's private offices, Xaviero expelled a long, low breath.

'Have your passport ready,' he instructed softly. 'A car will be sent to pick you up at ten tomorrow morning—'

'Xaviero, I have a new job.'

'Yes, I know that,' he said impatiently as he saw the red light of another phone begin to flash on his desk. 'I've had my people check it out.'

My people? For some reason the words jarred. It sounded scary—and more than a bit *controlling*. 'I can't just walk out and leave them in the lurch.'

'Don't worry—all that will be taken care of. The store will be adequately compensated and a replacement found for you, if necessary.'

He barely even needed to think about it, she realised. Such was his power and his influence that he could simply shift people around like chess pieces. He had done it first with Rupert and now he was doing it again. Could that be *good* for a person? Was it good for her to be at his beck and call like this? 'And I've moved. I'm not living where you think I'm living any more.'

'I know that, too. Cathy, these are just minor details which can easily be resolved.'

Minor details? These minor details were her *life*! Cathy swallowed. It sounded so humdrum to ask—but she needed to know, or risk making a fool of herself. 'And what…what shall I bring?'

'Bring very little.' There was a pause. 'All that will be taken care of as well.'

Again, that sense of utter influence and dominance—that newly emphatic timbre to his voice. Surely he had not sounded quite that oppressive in the past? Did that mean her stay was to be short? 'Xaviero, I—'

'Look, I told you—I can't talk now. It's… I'll see you tomorrow—there will be time enough then.' There was a pause. 'Goodbye, Cathy.'

She was left holding a buzzing receiver as he terminated the connection and when she'd replaced the receiver she didn't move for a moment or two. As if expecting her phone to ring again and for someone to say that it had all been a mistake. That the Prince had temporarily taken leave of his senses.

But no such phone call came, and instead Cathy realised that what he'd said must be true. Pulling herself together, she went into her bedroom and packed a small suitcase—hideously aware of the shortcomings of her meagre wardrobe.

She spent the rest of the evening cleaning the apartment and the following morning she was up pacing the floor, her stomach a knot of anxiety, when the car arrived. It was the same dark, bullet-proofed limousine which she'd ridden in with Xaviero on their one proper 'date' to the polo club. It seemed like an age ago. Another life.

They sped with miraculous ease through the traffic—never seeming to be challenged until Cathy noticed the diplomatic flag fluttering on the vast and shiny bonnet and realised why. And then on to an airfield where a private plane was waiting, along with several hefty-looking officials who scanned her passport—was it her imagination, or were they looking at her askance?—before whisking her aboard the luxury jet.

She refused most of the fancy foods and drinks offered by two sleek female cabin crew, and the journey passed Cathy by in something of a blur. She felt a bit as she'd done after a general anaesthetic when she'd had her tonsils removed—all whoozy and disorientated—and it wasn't until the plane began to descend towards a crescent-shaped island set in a sapphire sea that apprehension began to set in once more.

Her heart began to pound as the aircraft passed over deep green cypress forests towards a small airport. Would Xaviero be waiting there to meet her with some kind of explanation about why she had been rushed out here like this? She peered out of the porthole window at a small cluster of people who were assembled on the tarmac, presumably waiting for her to land. But she couldn't see any sign of him—just a large car with dark-tinted windows at the front of several other similar, assorted vehicles.

Warm, scented air washed over her as she walked carefully down the steps and onto the tarmac where a smart woman of around forty, dressed in cream linen, detached herself from the group and came towards her, hand outstretched in greeting.

'Catherine?' She smiled. 'We are delighted you are here. My name is Flavia Simoni and I am the wife of Prince Xaviero's political secretary. Did you have a pleasant flight?'

Cathy wanted to say to the woman that she was *never* called 'Catherine'—but maybe now wasn't the right time.

'It was fine. Thank you. How's Casimiro?' she asked, wondering if she'd imagined the momentary look of disapproval which crossed the woman's face.

'I am sure that the Prince Xaviero will wish to speak to you in person about his brother, the King,' Flavia replied coolly.

Yes, definitely disapproval. Cathy felt slightly desperate now—aware of the beads of sweat which were prickling her forehead and the sudden dawning that she hadn't realised how *hot* it would be. Surreptitiously wiping the back of her hand over her brow, she looked around. Surely he was here to meet her? Perhaps sitting in the back of one of those dark-windowed cars. 'And is he here? Xav—Prince Xaviero, I mean,' she amended hastily.

'Unfortunately, he is not. The Prince is tied up with affairs of state,' said Flavia. 'Which is why he asked me to accompany you to the palace. So if you would like to come with me, we'll waste no more time.'

As she slid onto the back seat Cathy tried desperately to smooth down a floral dress which looked so cheap when compared to Flavia's cool, creamy linen. A million questions warred in her head, but the one which screamed out with utter clarity was the most fundamental of all. Having flown her out here without any kind of explanation—*why on earth wasn't he here to meet her?*

She stared out of the window, trying to take in the beauty of this foreign land. Thick palm trees lined a surprisingly wide road—their succulent fronds outlined against a sky of breathtaking blue and the air was light from the glitter of sun on the distant sapphire sea. After a while, she could see the cluster of buildings in the distance and she leaned forward to get a closer look.

'We are approaching our capital city of Ghalazamba,' said Flavia, with a note of unmistakable pride in her voice. 'A city which has been ruled by the di Cesere family for centuries.'

Flavia's statement only served to increase Cathy's growing sense of unease. Yes, she knew that Xaviero was a prince, but, despite the fancy car and the discreet presence of his bodyguards, his royal status had not really intruded on the time they'd spent together in England. But *here*…why, it was as if the sheer magnitude of his royal inheritance had hit her for the very first time.

As they passed through the city walls Cathy thought the beautiful buildings looked like pictures she'd seen of Venice—while the dark, labyrinth lanes emphasised that she was essentially in an unknown and secretive place. But then everything became greener—she could discern a verdant sweep of unexpectedly lush grass through the tallest gates she had ever seen. Gates which gleamed a gold as bright as

Xaviero's eyes and which swung open to allow the car through.

'And this, the royal palace of Zaffirinthos,' announced Flavia quietly.

The palms of her hands growing clammy with nerves, Cathy stared up at a huge, stately white building with tall columns and elegant, arch-shaped windows. She was aware of unfamiliar trees and plants—flowers she'd never seen before—and the scent of their perfume was overpowering. There was a stately statue of a nymph standing in the centre of a fountain—a small globe held in her hands, over which cool water flowed, and Cathy wished she could go and splash some over her heated brow.

Gesturing to a sweep of marble stairs which lined the main entrance and was guarded by a row of solemn-faced men in uniform, Flavia indicated that Cathy should follow her. 'The Prince has requested that I take you immediately to his private office,' she said.

Cathy's heart began to race as, suddenly, a wave of uncertainty swept over her. *What was she doing here in this mighty and magnificent palace where, all around, inscrutable guards failed to meet her eyes?* But there was no time to think or to wonder because long marble corridors were echoing to the sound of their footsteps and minutes later she was being ushered into a room so elaborate and glittering that it momentarily took her breath away.

But only momentarily—because her attention was immediately drawn to the tall figure who stood by one of the long windows. His face and powerful body were shadowed by the light behind him, but just seeing him again made Cathy realise how much she had missed him and how she had longed and craved to feel his embrace.

'Xaviero!' she cried, and impetuously started to move towards him until the brief elevation of an imperious palm stopped her in her tracks and the words dried on her lips.

He stepped out of the shadows then and, with a shock, she could see that he had lost weight. The flesh was stretched tightly over the autocratic bones of his face and his golden eyes were darkened by lack of sleep. But more than that—they were cold and distant. Gleaming out a warning so distinct that he might as well have held up a placard saying: *Do not come near me.* The only thing she could compare it to was that time when he had told her that their affair was over and he was going to South America. Back then, as now, it had been as if he'd flicked a switch to make himself icily inaccessible—and a sudden feeling of foreboding made her heart miss a beat.

'It is good to see you again, Catherine,' he said, in a voice she'd never heard him use before. Cool and diplomatic—it made her feel as if she were little more than a stranger to him.

And Catherine? What was it with all this 'Catherine'? First Flavia and now him. Dazed by the sheer magnificence of her surroundings and more than a little intimidated by Xaviero's daunting presence, she stood before him mutely and waited for some kind of explanation which might clear this confusing fog she seemed to be standing in. 'It is good to see you too, Your Highness,' she said, echoing his formal tone.

Xaviero looked at her. Wearing some crumpled and cheap little dress, she could not have looked more out of place in the splendour of the palace setting and for a moment he wondered if he had undergone some kind of temporary insanity by bringing her out here.

But what choice did he have in a situation which showed no sign of ceasing? What was it they said? he thought bitterly. *Be careful what you wish for…*

'Flavia,' he said steadily, with barely a glance at the middle-aged aide. 'I wonder if you might give us a few moments?'

'Of course, Your Highness.' Flavia bobbed a smooth curtsey before exiting the room and quietly shutting the massive doors behind her.

And it was the curtsey which stirred a distant memory and shook Cathy out of her torpor. 'I thought you didn't like formality,' she said slowly.

He gave a grim kind of smile. 'Unfortunately, it has become a necessity I am fast learning to deal with. There are fairly rigid definitions of acceptable behaviour here—and you running across the room and hurling yourself into my arms in front of an aide isn't really one of them.'

The criticism stung—but how had she been expected to know the rules of royal protocol when all she had been trying to do was console him? 'How…how is your brother?'

The golden eyes seared through her. Could he trust her? *Really* trust her? And yet would he have brought her out here on this crazy mission if he did not? 'What I tell you is in strictest confidence.'

'Of course.'

'His condition remains unchanged. The King lies in a coma, unresponsive to all stimuli.' Xaviero's mouth thinned into a bleak line. 'He is alive and yet not alive—for he can engage none of the senses which really constitute living.'

She heard bitterness mixed with sadness in his voice and something else, too—something she couldn't put her finger on. 'I'm so sorry.'

'Yes. We're all sorry.'

She lifted her eyes to his, realising that he still

hadn't touched her—and that something in his body language was deeply forbidding, as if daring her to touch *him*. And she didn't. How could she after everything he'd just said? She stood there feeling as if he were nothing more than a distant stranger. He seemed like a man she had known briefly in another life—and yet she couldn't even imagine it now. It seemed impossible to think of him in her arms and in her little bed, making love to her and teaching her how to pleasure him. He looked cold, untouchable—like some gleaming golden statue.

'Xaviero,' she whispered. 'Why have you brought me here?'

By the shafts of his powerful thighs, Xaviero's fingers briefly flexed—a split second of unfamiliar indecision making him hesitate. Because the repercussions of what he was about to say were enormous. He regarded her steadily. Should he go through with it? *Could* he go through with it? And yet, did he really have any choice in the matter if he was to live any kind of tolerable life here on an island where his every move was watched and analysed? Drawing a deep breath, he stared down into the wide-spaced aquamarine eyes.

'I want you to marry me,' he said flatly.

CHAPTER EIGHT

CATHY suddenly experienced the strangest sensation—almost as if she had moved outside her body, and were now looking down on it. As if she were distanced and removed from the moment.

She could see the imposing physique of the Prince radiating power and privilege—and that slightly hunched woman in the crumpled floral dress must be her. She was staring up at him, an expression of disbelief on her face—as if she couldn't believe that such a man had just asked her to marry him. Her lips were dry and she couldn't utter a word—even if she'd had a clue how to reply.

'Cathy? Did you hear what I said?'

His voice interrupted the swirling confusion of her thoughts and brought her telescoping back into her own body with a shock. Swallowing down the sudden clamour of fear as her senses returned, she felt the cold prickle of sweat at her brow and prayed that she wouldn't do something foolish, like slide to the ground in a faint.

Yet her heart wasn't beating wildly with the exultant joy she might have expected. Wasn't it strange how something you'd longed for only in your wildest dreams could have the ring of the nightmare about it when it actually came true? This man—no, this *prince*—had flown her out to his Mediterranean island and just proposed marriage to her. Cathy's eyes searched the hard contours of his face, wanting him to repeat it—no, *needing* him to repeat it, for fear that she might be quietly going insane.

'I'm not sure that I did,' she said. 'Say it again.'

'I want you to marry me.'

Her voice was now little more than a hoarse whisper. 'But...*why*?'

'Because...' He knew the words she wanted—the words were traditional at such a time. Words of love and hopes for a shared future. But he couldn't do that. Xaviero wasn't blind to his faults—though the power afforded him by his position in society meant that they were always tolerated, even indulged—but he had never been a hypocrite and he wasn't going to start now. 'Because I need a wife.'

Need. It was an interesting choice of word and usually it implied some kind of emotional dependence—but Cathy suspected that it didn't mean the same for Xaviero as it did for other people. His face was nothing but a cool, dark mask of near-indifference. He wasn't exactly flinging his arms around her and telling her that she was the only woman in the world for him, was he? That his life would never be the same unless she said yes.

'Why?' she questioned again. 'I don't understand.'

Again, he chose his words with care. The truth was vital, yes—but how much of it could she take? And yet if he were anything other than completely candid with her—might she not in future turn round in that hysterical way that women sometimes had when life didn't turn out the way they wanted it to, and accuse him of having tricked her?

'Because…' The lump in his throat momentarily restricted his speech. 'Because my brother lies insensible in his hospital bed and thus is powerless to act in the interests of his people. It is an impossible situation which cannot continue and I have been charged to govern my country as Prince Regent until he recovers.'

'*Until?*' Cathy seized on the single word. 'You mean there's a chance he *will* recover?'

His eyes narrowed. He had forgotten her native intelligence which seemed to shine through despite her formal lack of education. Had he implied that Casimiro's prognosis was hopeful? '*If* he recovers,' he allowed unwillingly and then met the question which clouded her brilliant aquamarine eyes. 'The doctors think it unlikely. They say that he could lie in this vegetative state for years. I am to be sworn in as Prince Regent—and if I am to rule, then I need a woman at my side.'

To help and support him? she wondered—as her heart gave a sudden leap of hope. To be his solace and his comfort in times of need? Wouldn't she gladly do all that—and more—for this complex and compelling man? Wouldn't she be honoured and thrilled to stand by his side? Trying not to let the sudden rise of happiness show on her face, she clasped her hands together. 'Do you?'

He nodded. '*Sì*. The people are obviously unsettled by what has happened. But a new Princess would give them hope—something bright to lighten the gloom of the accident and the dark days which have followed. Someone to open their hospitals and visit their schools.' There was a pause while his golden eyes gleamed out a different message entirely. 'While I cannot live without the physical comfort which only a woman can provide. A comfort which you provide so exquisitely,' he said, his voice growing husky with memory. 'As we both know only too well.'

Somehow Cathy kept her face from crumpling. What had she been expecting—words of *love*? Or at least words which contained *some* kind of affection, along with hope for a shared future.

Instead, he had presented her with the option of visiting schools and warming his bed at night! Was he expecting her to eagerly snatch at his offer—the way she had greedily fallen into bed with him? Well, she would match his cool words with her own response.

'But why me?' she queried. 'Why not a woman more suitable for a prince—someone high-born and not a humble chambermaid?'

Xaviero nodded, pleased with the dispassionate nature of her question—because surely that boded well for the future. 'Because I know the identity of every eligible woman on the island—and have no wish to marry any of them. But neither do I have the time to go trawling the world in search of a more…' He shrugged as he met her eyes, but he would not shrink from what was, essentially, the truth. 'A more *suitable* candidate of aristocratic breeding. And of course you have one essential qualification for the role, Cathy—one which I can vouch for myself.'

'My virginity?' she guessed slowly.

'Of course.' Remembering the afternoon she

had lost it, he felt the beat of desire and longed to take her in his arms right then. To lose himself there in the sweetest way possible and to temporarily rid himself of some of the dark weight of expectation which now fell on his shoulders. But he dared not touch her. Not yet. 'So…' He raised his dark brows. 'Your thoughts on the matter?'

If only he had kissed her or hugged her instead of asking the question in such a cold-blooded way. If he had let physical affection masquerade as love—then wouldn't it have made everything easier? But he was still standing away from her—only a few feet, it was true, but it might as well have been a million miles. *Think straight, Cathy*, she urged herself. *Because this is very important—for both of you. And if you are to give his unbelievable proposal any serious consideration, then you must be in full possession of the facts.*

And that meant remaining as detached as he was.

'So my innocence is the sole reason for this fairy-tale proposal?'

Xaviero gave a quick smile. Was she trying to shock him with her sudden bluntness? 'I think you underestimate your petite, blonde beauty, *mia tesoro*,' he demurred softly. 'Though our marriage would of course be impossible if you had been intimate with other men. But it is your biddable nature which was equally important in helping me come to my decision.'

Cathy stilled. 'What…what are you talking about?'

'It is one of your most commendable qualities—the fact that you are so wonderfully compliant,' he murmured and he began to walk across the room towards her. 'Such a wonderfully old-fashioned trait and it is *because* you are not from aristocracy that you are in possession of it. I watched you begin to learn about sex with an enthusiasm and an aptitude which was thrilling to behold. Your eagerness to please and to improve bodes well, Cathy—and can be applied to other fields outside the bedroom.'

'Compliant?' she repeated weakly, because now he was before her—his glorious face in close-up, his own distinctive scent invading her senses.

'Yes—compliant. You are like a blank canvas

on which I can paint whatever I like. Someone who will learn to be the perfect Princess, just as you have learnt to be the perfect lover. Few women are as teachable as you, *mia bella* Cathy. Now come here—'

His voice had dipped and Cathy heard the raw hunger in it—but she stood stiff and unmoving when he took her into his arms. *Say no*, she silently urged herself. *Tell him what he can do with his insulting request. Tell him that you're more than just an ex-virgin who learns quickly and will grab at anything he offers you.*

'Cathy,' he murmured, touching the tousled fall of her hair as he had been longing to do from the moment she had entered the room, tangling his fingers in its silken spill. 'Sweet, sweet Cathy.'

She tried to fight it, but desire was proving far stronger than pride—and hadn't she hungered for his touch for so long? Hadn't he hovered on the periphery of her every waking thought for each moment they'd been apart—reminding her of how totally he could captivate her?

She had thought that she had tasted the last of

him, and couldn't ever have envisaged that she would be in his arms again. But now she was, and it was even better than she remembered— obliterating everything but a hot and urgent desire. He was smoothing his palms down the side of her head, stroking her hair as if she were a cat. Each of his thumbs was now tracing an outline on each side of her lips, sending them into a helpless tremble. It was a fervent and curiously innocent gesture and it was almost her undoing. 'Xaviero—'

'Kiss me,' he urged, his voice suddenly raw. 'Kiss me as you've been wanting to kiss me since you walked in here. But do it now for we do not have long—and then I must have your answer.'

Pride made her ask and she prayed that her eagerness didn't show. 'You still haven't told me wh-what's in it for me.'

Should he tempt her with diamonds and palaces? Or something more potent still? The inexplicable something which had sizzled between them right from the start. 'This,' he said roughly as his mouth drove down to meet hers.

Later she wondered that if she'd had the strength not to let him kiss her, whether her answer might have been different. But she was too weak to resist and just one touch was like lighting the touchpaper on her dormant passion. And hadn't he had that power over her from the very moment he had first walked into her life— the man in denim with the lazy smile? Hungrily, she clung to him as his lips began to plunder hers and she gasped as he pulled her roughly against him so that she could be in no doubt about the powerful strength of his arousal.

Cathy moaned softly. If he had stripped her bare and taken her there, without formality on the marble floor of the elaborate room, she would have let him—welcomed it even, for then he would have been simply a man again, without all the trappings of his royal title. But he suddenly terminated the kiss, his golden eyes almost black as they scoured her face, his breathing as ragged as if he had just been running a race.

'You will be my bride,' he stated, necessity forcing him to swallow down the urge to quickly join with her sweet, supple body, and then he put his lips to her ear. 'Won't you?'

And despite the misgivings which ran as deep as her desire, Cathy knew that she couldn't say no to that soft, urgent entreaty. This renewed contact with him had made her realise just what she'd been missing, how much she had ached for him during his absence—and the thought of leaving him tore at her heart like a rusty nail. It was true, he wasn't offering her what men usually offered when they asked a woman to marry them—but he was offering himself.

And wasn't that enough?

Couldn't she make it enough?

'Yes, Xaviero,' she said slowly, her heart thudding beneath one swollen breast. 'I will be your bride.'

CHAPTER NINE

IT WAS, by necessity, a quiet and hasty wedding. With the young King lying hovering between life and death in a hospital bed, any lavish display of celebration would have been seen as being in extremely bad taste.

In the event, Cathy found the low-key tone of the event a relief. Imagine if it had been a full-blown royal wedding, she thought—attended by all the world's top dignitaries and politicians? The kind of nuptials which had apparently been enjoyed by Xaviero's own parents and which had been splashed over glossy magazines the world over. How on earth would she have managed to pretend that her own union was all for real—and that her royal groom was madly in love with her—if there were battalions of cameras around? Until she reminded herself that she wouldn't *be* here if it were a 'normal' royal wedding—because Xaviero wouldn't have needed a bride in such a hurry.

Flavia was assigned to help Cathy settle into the beautiful and closely guarded house within the palace compound which was to be her home until the marriage—and to school her in the automatic changes which the ceremony would bring.

'You understand that with the making of your vows, you will automatically become a princess?' the older woman asked.

'Yes.'

'And that in future, you will be known as Catherine.'

Cathy smiled. 'I prefer Cathy, if you don't mind.'

Flavia's expression hadn't changed. 'Actually, that won't be possible,' she said apologetically. 'The Prince Regent has ordered all your stationery to bear the name Catherine.'

For someone whose identity had already been in crisis, this was the final straw—and Cathy went marching off to the Prince Regent's room. And then was humiliatingly forced to endure an hour-long wait while Xaviero finished off with some government business before he could see her.

When she was eventually ushered into his office, he took one frowning look at her and then dismissed all his aides until they were alone together—something which had not happened since the day when he had proposed marriage to her.

His eyes narrowed as he indicated the seat in front of him, knowing that he had a meeting with the transport secretary in half an hour and a whole stack of reading to get through before then in order to get his head round the new road plans. For the first time in his life, he was realising that he couldn't use his immense wealth to delegate—that the buck really did stop with him. And that maybe this kind of power wasn't all it was cracked up to be… 'Sit down,' he said.

Distractedly, she shook her head. 'I don't want to sit down!'

He let that go. For now. Was the frustration of

being apart so much getting to her as much as it was to him? If that were the case, then he would forgive her discourtesy—but she would have to learn soon enough that he would not tolerate being spoken to like that. Not even by his wife. 'Something has upset you?'

'I won't change my name!'

He laid down his fountain pen and studied her, a nerve beginning to work in his cheek. 'You have interrupted my busy morning schedule to talk to me about a *name*?' he questioned in disbelief.

Couldn't he see that it was more than just the matter of a name? That she was left feeling like a puppet which was having its strings jerked— and that now even her identity had been torn from her? 'I won't change it, Xaviero.'

'It is not a question of choice. You must.'

'*Must?*'

Compliance had been one of the main reasons he had selected her as his wife—but she was displaying none of that compliance now. Xaviero's mouth hardened. If she was to learn the hard lesson of obedience to her royal husband, then was it not better she did so as soon as possible?

'Yes, must,' he bit out, ignoring yet another phone sending out its silent, flashing demand. 'Which part of the word don't you understand?'

Cathy flinched. 'Am I…?' She was aware that her voice was trembling—but that was less to do with her sudden sense of powerlessness and more to do with the gleam of quiet fury which was emanating from the golden eyes. 'Am I allowed to know why?'

He didn't want to hurt her, but she had pushed him into a corner and she would learn not to do so again. 'Because Catherine is the name of a possible future Queen, while "Cathy" is the name of a—'

She swallowed as the great gulf of inequality stretched between them like a black chasm. 'A chambermaid?'

'Precisely.' He saw the aquamarine eyes begin to take on a suspiciously bright glitter and he felt a momentary wave of irritation. His brother might be dying and she was making a fuss about a damned *name*? Appeasement did not come easily to him, but with an effort he sought to embrace it now. 'Look,' he said, in as placating a tone as he had ever used. 'Catherine is a very pretty name. It suits you. Is it such a big thing to ask?'

Maybe it wasn't—but Cathy was already reeling from the list of 'dos' and 'don'ts' she'd been given by Flavia. Don't stand up unless you want the entire room to follow suit. Don't spend too long in any line-up. Don't forget that everyone who tries to make your acquaintance will have their own agenda—and will try to use their royal connection to better themselves. But the one which had scared her the most was: *Don't trust anyone without first running it past the palace.* No wonder Xaviero was so cynical.

She had spent the morning with a dress designer who had been unable to hide her faint surprise when she'd seen Cathy's existing clothes—before revealing her planned designs for her new, royal wardrobe with the air of a magician producing a rabbit from a hat. And Cathy had looked at all the different clothes she was going to need with a sense of wonder. The brand-new outfits she would require when she took her place in royal life would have excited the heart of most young women. But she was left wondering whether all traces of the real Cathy were going to be completely eradicated by her makeover. And now this.

'Maybe I would have liked to have been consulted about the name change *before* it was decided,' she said, in a small voice.

'And you will be in future,' he assured her suavely. 'I promise.'

She felt like a child being placated with a spoonful of sugar after an unexpected dose of particularly nasty medicine. It seemed so long since Xaviero had actually *touched* her. And wasn't that part of the trouble—that she was left feeling insubstantial, as if she didn't really exist any more?

'And I really want to kiss you,' she said boldly.

He felt the hot jerk of arousal as he got up from behind the desk and advanced towards her, his face darkening with frustration. 'You think I don't? You think I don't lie awake at night realising that you're on the other damned side of the compound surrounded by guards? Why, I am so hot for you that I hardly dare trust myself in your company,' he groaned, before pulling her into his arms and kissing her with an intensity which made him think very seriously about locking the door.

Instantly, she began to melt beneath the seeking heat of his lips—feeling the warm pooling of her blood, the faint tremble of her knees. 'Xaviero,' she breathed against his mouth. 'I want you.'

Splaying his hand greedily over the curve of one magnificent breast and feeling its bursting tightness, he found himself wondering whether there would be time to…to…

And then one of the phones on the desk began to ring and silently he cursed her for inflicting desire on him before so vital a meeting. This was madness! For a moment back there, he'd actually been contemplating…

'You see?' he demanded heatedly. 'Now you have driven me into a state of intense longing!'

'And that was wr-wrong?'

'Of course it was wrong!' He looked down into her darkened eyes and saw the way her lips now quivered with uncertainty. For a moment his voice softened as he traced a featherlight outline over their trembling surface. 'You must learn that duty always comes before desire and we can't do this, *mia bella*. Not now—and certainly not here.'

His soft censure sliced through her like a knife and Cathy's hand reached out to a nearby chair to steady herself on its gilded support. Had she made a complete fool of herself—trying to seduce him away from his frantic workload? 'I'm sorry.'

He shook his head impatiently. 'It's forgotten— but if you embrace the rule from the beginning, then there won't be any need to apologise. There are certain protocols to be observed and one of them is that it is unwise for us to be alone together before the wedding. We certainly can't make love without causing a national scandal and that is something I am not prepared to do in the current circumstances—no matter how much I want you. The wedding takes place the day after tomorrow—

so you won't have much longer to wait. Do you think you can hold out until then?'

Cathy felt the sting of colour to her cheeks. 'There's no need to make me sound like some kind of…of…sex maniac.'

Softly, he laughed. 'Oh, I'm not knocking it, *mia bella*. Your unashamed eagerness is one of the very things which makes you so very irresistible. It's just a question of timing.' His eyes glittered as they raked over her flushed face. 'And think about how good it's going to feel, mmm?' He went back behind the sanctuary of his desk and picked up the golden fountain pen before flicking her another quick glance. 'Oh, and in the future, you are to be known as Catherine—is that understood?'

He had waited until she was soft, vulnerable—and then he had driven his point home with ruthless disregard for her feelings. Cathy bit her lip. But what could she do, other than agree?

Because by then a whole train of events had been set in motion and she knew that it was too late to stop them, even if she wanted to. And when it boiled down to it—did she really want to escape from all this, and, more importantly, from Xaviero himself? To do what? Go back to London and her job in the bookshop? Deep down she knew that there was no contest—even if instinct told her that she was laying herself open to possible heartache.

And so it was that Catherine Helen Burton married the Prince Xaviero Vincente Caius di Cesere in the exquisite chapel within the palace compound and became his Princess. The only people present were the Prime Minister, the Chief Minister of Justice and their partners as well as Flavia and her husband, Marco—the Prince's aide.

Naturally, there was no one from Cathy's side and it seemed that this was another point in her favour—that she arrived unencumbered by any emotional baggage. Thus there was no chance of potential embarrassment from loud-mouthed re-latives—because she didn't have any. No kiss-and-tell stories or embarrassing photographs dredged up from the past. In fact, no press were present, either—although a brief statement was to be issued to the world's media afterwards.

Cathy wore a pearl-coloured dress of silk chiffon, ornamented by a short, lace bolero jacket worn during the service, which added a touch of formality. She had wanted something knee-length and more relaxed—something which seemed more appropriate for the occasion. But in this, as in so much else, she was overruled. As Flavia crisply informed her— princesses didn't wear day-dresses when they married. They wore fairy-tale dresses which little girls would drool over when the photos appeared in the island's newspaper the following day.

So Cathy tried to appreciate the thousands of tiny seed pearls which had been sewn into the bodice and filmy skirt of the dress and which gleamed as she moved. And to acknowledge that the pearls and diamonds which glittered in the tiara which adorned her carefully coiffured hair were *real* jewels. How many women would long to wear something this magnificent? Yet their cold brilliance was slightly intimidating as well as beautiful—their weight as heavy as the burden of expectation which she knew hovered over her.

But she would be a *good* Princess, she told herself fiercely. She would care for her Prince in any way that he would let her—and she would use whatever talents she had to try to make the people of Zaffirinthos happy.

There was no triumphant peel of bells as they emerged from the chapel into the bright sunshine and she wondered whether there might be a public kiss to seal the union. But there was not. Just the golden gleam of his eyes as he looked down at her.

'So, Catherine,' he said softly. 'Princess of Zaffirinthos. How does that feel?'

'It feels unreal,' she admitted with a whisper and saw the brief shuttering of his face.

'All royal life is unreal.' He gave a short laugh. 'That is both its attraction and its danger.'

'Its *danger*?' she questioned shakily.

Lifting one olive-skinned hand, he gestured at the splendour which surrounded them. 'Of course. Sometimes people who are not born to it find it incredibly restrictive. Or they fall in love with the heady sense of power it bestows. Few remain immune to its lure. Can't you see the danger in that, Cathy?'

'I…suppose so.' She wanted him to tell her not to worry, that it was all going to be okay—especially today, of all days. She wanted to feel part of everything—but most of all she wanted to feel part of *him* in the way that all new brides were supposed to. Her fingers dug into the tight white roses of her bouquet. 'But I'd prefer to think about happier matters on my wedding day.'

He looked down at her. With her pale hair caught up in a sophisticated chignon and threaded with glittering jewels, she looked incandescent. Already, the image of the simple little chambermaid she had once been was fading—though her naïve statement reminded him that, essentially, she was the same woman underneath. 'Yes, of course you do. So come on. Big smile—and then let's go and say hello to the staff.'

All the palace personnel were lined up along the marble steps to greet the newly-weds and

Cathy was grateful that Flavia had told her to stop and chat only every few places—otherwise they would have been there all day. But she saw a couple of crestfallen faces from the younger maids she didn't actually get to speak to—and she determined to make their acquaintance on another occasion. Because hadn't she been there, where they were—a small, anonymous face looking out at all the splendour as the moneyed people went by?

Suddenly, Cathy felt a pang for the old life— the life she had left behind. One where feelings were allowed precedence over rules, and where it would have been perfectly acceptable for a new bride to fling her arm around her husband's neck and to kiss him.

The wedding breakfast was held in what she had learned was the smallest and most intimate of the three dining halls—though intimacy was not a word which married well with such a room. How could it when every piece of cutlery they used was made of solid gold and studded with rubies? Even the crystal glass containing priceless wine was so heavy that she needed to use two hands to pick it up.

And Cathy suddenly realised that she had nothing to say! Not unless she started advising the noble assembly how to make a bed—or the best way to fold sheets—and Flavia had tacitly advised her not to dwell on her former life. Her words and her thoughts seemed to have dried up, leaving her feeling empty. Not that anyone seemed to mind. It was clearly Xaviero who was of prime importance. Xaviero whose jokes they laughed at and Xaviero whose observations were met with nodding interest.

Cathy sat listening, absorbing everything she heard—trying to learn as much about her new royal life as she could. But the meal seemed to drag on and on—course after course of it—all amazing little delicacies, most of which she'd never tasted before and were much too rich to lay comfortably in a stomach already churned up with nerves. Especially when all she really wanted was for Xaviero to take her in his arms and to kiss away all her fears and insecurity.

Yet despite the fact that they were newly wed, they were still surrounded by onlookers and protocol. She tried sending him looks of appeal across the glittering table—and was it her imagination, or did he simply ignore her silent entreaty?

By the time the meal was finished she was a mass of insecurity, but consoled herself with the sight of her new husband as he stood up. In his dark naval uniform awash with medals as golden as his eyes, he looked so tall and so handsome. And in that moment Cathy simply felt an immense and quiet pride that she had married such a man.

It didn't matter what had gone before—it was the now which mattered, and soon she would be locked in his arms again. Her bare skin would be close to his in a way she had hardly dared remember, for fear that it would never happen again. But tonight it most definitely would. Hadn't they always been magic in bed together—and wouldn't her pleasure only be enhanced by knowing that she was now legally his wife? She could show him love in the privacy of their bedchamber and Xaviero would learn to accept it—maybe even one day to return it.

Slanting him a demure smile, she rose to her feet—smoothing down the silk chiffon of her wedding dress and imagining him peeling it from her body very soon.

He walked over to her side and offered her his arm as he took her over to the window, for he had not been oblivious to her pale fidgeting through-out the meal. 'You seem a little distracted, Catherine,' he murmured.

Unseeingly, she gazed out at the perfectly manicured palace gardens and told herself not to react. If Catherine he wanted her to be—then Catherine she would be. Hadn't she learnt her lesson over *that* particular quibble?

'Do I? Well, it's been a pretty overwhelming experience,' she answered truthfully, and then lowered her voice so that only he could hear her next remark—because surely a new bride was allowed a little coquetry with her husband, no matter how exalted his position. 'And I just can't wait to be alone with you.'

'Neither can I.' He didn't miss a beat as he saw her lips part. 'But you must be patient for a little longer.'

'P-patient?' She turned her eyes up to him in bewilderment. 'You mean there is some other sort of c-celebration we must attend?'

'Hardly a celebration,' said Xaviero, his voice hardening. 'Now that you are my wife, protocol demands that you must meet my brother, the King. When the meal is ended, we will be driven to the hospital.'

'Y-your brother? But…'

He raised his dark brows. 'But what?'

'Your brother's in a coma, Xaviero.' Tiredly, she shrugged her shoulders—aware of the weight of the pearl-encrusted bodice and the tiara still in her hair. 'Does it…does it have to be today?'

'You mean, he won't know or won't care *when* I introduce him to my new bride—that we could wait a year and he wouldn't notice?'

Hearing the condemnation in his voice, she lowered her own. 'I didn't mean that at all. It's just that you look exhausted—it's obvious you've been under a lot of strain since you came back and took over. Would it be so very wrong if we spent a little time on our own tonight—and went to see Casimiro tomorrow?'

Didn't the guilt which was churning inside him make him want to lash out? 'Is it too much to ask,' he questioned, in a voice of silken danger, 'that you wait a little longer to satisfy your sexual appetite?'

She wanted to gasp out her outrage, to vehemently deny his softly uttered accusation—but, of course, she could not. Not when there were the island's most important dignitaries on the other side of the room, no doubt trying to ignore the fact that the newly-weds seemed to be having some kind of disagreement.

'I wouldn't have put it quite like that,' she said, her calm voice belying the painful scudding of her heart. 'And you know I'm longing to meet your brother.'

'Then why make all this fuss?' he questioned softly.

Somehow he had managed to twist her words and leave her feeling inadequate—as if she had failed him on every level. The first test of royal life, and she had somehow flunked it.

Pausing only to change from her wedding gown into something more suitable for hospital visiting, Cathy joined Xaviero in the back of the limousine for a tense journey across the city as she nervously twisted the new gold wedding band round and round on her finger.

But all her own insecurities were banished when they were ushered into the intensive-care room at the top of the high-tech building, to a room dominated by a white bed which for one awful moment almost resembled a bier. Her fingers flew to her lips and she bit back a little cry of distress.

For there lay the King. His eyes were closed and his muscles wasted through inactivity—but he was still recognisably a formidable figure with the same high slash of autocratic cheekbones as his brother. At well over six feet, he seemed to dwarf the narrow bed on which he lay and the deep, hoarse sound of his breathing echoed heart-breakingly through the room. Cathy looked at all

the medical paraphernalia of tubes and resusci-
tation equipment which surrounded him and had
never felt so helpless in her life. That a fine, fit
young man could be struck down like this…

And then she glanced over at Xaviero, and as
his tortured features burnt themselves into her
vision her heart clenched. He looked *haunted*,
she thought guiltily. No wonder he had been so
tetchy and so ill at ease with her. How must it feel
for him to see his brother lying there like that and
to be unable to do anything to help him, for all
his power and his position? And there she had
been—petulant about a name-change and
because she'd barely had any time alone with
him. A shudder racked her slender frame and for
a moment their eyes met in a shared moment of
silent pain.

'Casimiro,' said Xaviero heavily. 'I would like
you to meet my wife.'

And Cathy went through the motions of
sinking in a low curtsey. The head nurse had
advised her that the King might be able to hear
her, and that she should talk to him. And so,

shrugging off any feelings of self-consciousness, she sat and told the stricken monarch how happy she was to have married into his family and how she would do everything in her power to be a good princess. She found herself searching his inert, cold features for some kind of reaction— *any* kind of reaction. Could he understand anything she was saying to him? How terrible if his mind was locked in some frustrating prison— hearing everything and yet unable to respond.

By the time they left, a small crowd had gathered outside the hospital and Cathy was aware of the flash of a camera exploding in her face as Xaviero's security ushered them through to the car.

But once the powerful vehicle had moved off, her new husband reached out and pulled her close to him, staring down into her too-white face. 'I have been harsh with you, Cathy,' he said bitterly. 'Can you forgive me?'

'It…it doesn't matter.'

'Oh, but it does.'

'No, I have been putting my own concerns first,'

she whispered. 'Instead of realising all the respon-
sibilities which have been pressing down on you.'

He pushed her hair back from her cheek.
'Having you so close—and yet unable to touch
you—has been driving me half crazy with desire.'
His mouth softened into a smile tinged with
sadness. 'And you were brilliant with my brother.'

Basking beneath the unexpected compliment
and sinking into the longed-for warmth of his
embrace, Cathy found herself wanting to smooth
away those hard lines of strain from his formidable features. 'Does he get many visitors?'

All Xaviero wanted to do was to block out the
nightmare image of what they had just seen, but her
eyes were dark with a question he had no right to
ignore. 'We have no other living relatives.' He
shrugged. 'I go, when I have time…although every
second is now planned out for me, as you know, so
it is not as often as it should be. And, of course, I
do not find it as easy to talk to him as you just did.'

'That's because women are better at that kind
of thing.'

'Are they?' He allowed himself a brief smile.

'And naturally, the King's security and privacy is paramount, which means that no other visitors are permitted—not even his aides.'

Cathy thought about Casimiro's terrible loneliness and isolation, lying there with only the nurses going about their daily duties of helping keep him alive, and she bit her lip. 'Could I…could *I* go and visit him—would that be all right? I mean, I'm a relative now, aren't I?'

Xaviero looked into her shimmering blue eyes, taken aback by her tentative request—since a desire to visit the sickbay would not have been a request made by any of his past lovers. 'I don't see any reason why not,' he said gruffly.

'Then I'll ask Flavia to sort it out.'

He pulled her properly into his arms at last—and the sweet, fresh smell of her after the sterility of the hospital bay made him want to weep for all the joys his brother had lost. 'Oh, Cathy,' he said as he stared down at the uncertainty written on her trembling lips, wanting her to wipe some of the pain away with the tenderness of her touch. 'Cathy, Cathy, Cathy.'

Trembling with the pent-up emotion of all that had happened, she paid no heed to the fact that he had rebuffed her more than once. She was just empowered by a need which matched the naked hunger in his eyes and her arms reached up to lock themselves around his neck while their lips collided in a kiss. She heard the small ragged sigh which escaped him and felt the beat of his heart so close against her own. 'Xaviero,' she whispered.

'I want you,' he declared unevenly.

And, oh, how she wanted him. Back in a suite decorated with fragrant white roses, Cathy let him carry her straight to the bed, where he began undressing her with a sudden urgency.

'You haven't carried me over the threshold,' she teased.

'You want to go outside and come in again?' he demanded, lifting his head from her breasts, which he was baring—button by button—his eyes almost jet-black with desire.

Terrified of tempting a fate that had kept them segregated since she'd arrived and too transfixed by the shivers of desire which were skating inexorably over her skin, Cathy shook her head. 'No,' she whispered. 'I just want you.'

'Then you shall have me, *mia bella*. All night long, I am yours.' Making a sound a little like a low growl, Xaviero stripped the clothes from her body almost ruthlessly, his fingers and his lips re-acquainting themselves so deliciously with her flesh that she immediately choked out a little gasp of pleasure.

But that first time of making love as man and wife was not the slow coupling she might have hoped for. It was wild, almost primeval—though no less thrilling because of that. And the pleasure was exquisitely sharpened by abstinence. Yet it felt as if he was using the sex as some kind of catharsis to exercise unknown demons. Sobbing out his name as Xaviero shuddered inside her, Cathy clung to him as he breathed something in Italian against her damp skin.

'I've…I've missed you,' she said eventually.

Lazily, he turned onto his side, his finger tracing an undulating line from hip to breast, where it lingered and teased the rosy little tip until she gave a moan of pleasure. 'And I have missed *this*…' Letting the hand now splay luxuriantly over the silken globe of her bottom, he felt much of the strain and tension dissolving in that soft, sensual touch. 'You are…*sensational*,' he breathed.

'Am—am I?'

'I'd forgotten quite how much,' he declared unsteadily.

Wordlessly, they made love again and when it was over Cathy lay there staring up at the ceiling as her heartbeats gradually began to slow—not wanting to disturb a moment of the perfect harmony she felt. But as her own pleasure began to fade she felt a strange foreboding creep in to replace it. They were close, yes—but only physically close. The sense of oneness she had longed for had so far failed to materialise. Was she being greedy or unrealistic in expecting it to happen so soon? Or was she foolish in hoping that it might happen at all?

All night long, I am yours, he had said.

And for the rest of the time, what then?

CHAPTER TEN

THE next weeks were spent immersing herself in the art of being a princess—and Cathy was endlessly grateful for the adaptability she'd learnt while working at the hotel. Seamlessly slipping between chambermaiding and receptionist duties, she had been able to turn her hand to just about anything—and these were skills which proved invaluable in her new life.

And didn't throwing herself into her new role help her paper over the cracks in her marriage?

Busying herself with tasks befitting a brand-new royal helped Cathy forget that her worst fears were being realised, day by day. And that the ice-cold heart of her new husband could not be thawed, no matter how much tenderness or passion she showed him in their bed. Only at night did he let his guard down—but the ardent lover he became crumbled into nothing but a memory by morning. The mask of his regency was assumed as soon as his valet began laying out his clothes and he became a distant stranger once more.

It was as if she had no real part in his daily life—when he treated her with the undemonstrative civility he might show one of his aides. She was never allowed to show affection, nor to disturb him—and if she wanted to speak to him, she had to make an appointment like everyone else! Reminding herself that she had been chosen as his wife primarily because she would accept such conditions, she resolved to say nothing. And, like generations of women before her, Cathy played down the shortcomings in her relationship by reaching outside it for fulfilment.

Her days were spent organising her new office and deciding on what staff she would need to help her. There were posts for a private secretary, assistant secretaries and ladies-in-waiting as well as a hairdresser and a language coach. Although

English and Greek were taught in all the schools, Cathy had started to study Italian, which was the main language spoken on Zaffirinthos. From being a non-academic child herself at school, suddenly she could see the point in learning, if it actually had some kind of *purpose*.

And Xaviero's aides were proposing a grand joint tour of the island to introduce her to the people—even though the dark cloud of Casimiro's continuing coma meant that they were reluctant to pin down a date. But by then Cathy had started to visit the King on a regular basis and found that increased exposure to the inert figure on the white bed made his incapacity seem far less shocking than it had done at first.

She found herself actually looking forward to the visits—at least they made her feel as if she was being properly useful. She soon got to know all the nurses, who—once they'd stopped viewing her with a certain suspicion—soon started to warm to her. Because here, in this stark and bleak setting, all status and privilege seemed completely irrelevant.

Each day Cathy would sit with the King, while a bodyguard stood keeping his own vigil behind the bullet-proofed glass which had been specially installed. She found herself telling him about her blundering attempts to learn Italian and about how much all the staff at the palace talked about him and missed him. She described her little garden in England and how she hoped her tenants were looking after it properly.

And despite her own increasing loneliness, she tried to do what she had promised herself from the very beginning—to be a good wife to Xaviero, even though their time together was so restricted. Her foolish heart leapt with pleasure whenever they had a joint meeting scheduled, when they would sit at opposite ends of a long, polished table while their aides tossed out subjects for discussion. Or, briefly, they might exchange smiles if their respective retinues happened to pass each other along the wide, marble corridors of the palace.

They were rarely alone, except in bed when they would fall into each other's arms as if their lives depended on it. And in the pleasure that followed, Cathy couldn't bring herself to spoil the moment with a litany of complaints about how little they saw of each other. Maybe it was the same for every royal wife—one of the downsides behind the supposed fairy tale of privilege. In a way, with her limited access to him, she still felt a bit like a mistress—despite the bright band of gold on her finger and the royal crest which adorned her notepaper.

At meal times, there were always members of staff hovering silently in the background, pretending not to listen but watching carefully for any sign that the royal couple might require something—leaving Cathy to eat rather self-consciously, worried that her table manners might not be up to scratch. Perhaps that might explain why the waistbands on some of her dresses had become a little loose of late.

'You've lost weight,' said Xaviero one evening as she was dressing for a formal dinner arranged for a visiting Italian dignitary.

'Have I?' she questioned. And if her voice

sounded a little dazed, it was because she was still reeling from the fact that Xaviero was here—in her dressing room. He had wandered in to ask her to fix his cufflinks—a ridiculously simple and yet oddly intimate request which had left her feeling slightly flustered, until she had gathered her thoughts together enough to realise why.

Because they didn't *do* intimacy—not unless it was in the purely sexual sense. Xaviero had a valet to do his cufflinks. A tailor to measure his clothes. Aides he could confide in, and question about current affairs. Chefs to prepare his meals. He didn't need a wife in the way that other men did. His wife was an accessory—a compliant woman who was fast learning to be a competent princess.

'You know you have,' he said as he slowly circled her, like a predator eyeing up his victim. 'That dress fitted you perfectly the last time you wore it.'

'Only a few pounds,' said Cathy. 'And I'm… I'm surprised you noticed.'

Xaviero's eyes narrowed, allowing his gaze to drift over the creamy décolletage which was displayed to perfection by the soft sheen of the scarlet gown she wore. His voice thickened and he felt the familiar kick of lust. 'I notice everything about your magnificent body, *mia bella*—and you certainly don't need to lose any weight.'

'I wasn't trying to.'

She looked strained, he thought. The slight weight loss had made her cheekbones appear sharp and slanted, so that her face looked all eyes. Was she doing too much? Driving herself too hard in her attempts to fit in—attempts which hadn't gone unnoticed. Hadn't the court already expressed approval of her induction into the di Cesere family—despite initial misgivings about the wisdom of his hasty marriage to such a woman?

'Would you like a weekend away?' he questioned suddenly.

Cathy finished clipping in a diamond earring and met his eyes in the mirror, her heart beginning to thud with hope. A weekend away? Maybe like the honeymoon they'd never had? She turned round in the chair, a smile on her face as she beamed up at him. 'Oh, Xaviero—I'd love it! Do you really mean it?'

'Why not?' His lips curved into a speculative smile. She had been remarkably modest in her outgoings—in spite of him giving her carte blanche to spend his fortune as the mood took her. In fact, as far as he knew she had asked for nothing. If she had been trying to impress him with her restraint, then she had succeeded admirably—and maybe now was the time to reward her. 'You and Flavia could fly to Milan,' he suggested softly. 'Buy yourself something from the latest collections.'

It felt like a slap to the face but Cathy's smile didn't waver. How quickly she had become skilled at the royal art of never giving away your feelings by your facial expression. 'Flavia?' she echoed.

'*Sì*. The two of you get well, don't you?'

''Well, yes, we do—but that isn't the point. I thought you meant us…the two of *us*.'

He frowned. 'And how precisely would that happen, Cathy?' he questioned drily. 'Would someone magically step in to fill my shoes while I'm away? I am a busy man.'

With fingers which were trying not to tremble,

she turned back to the mirror and pretended to fuss with her hair. She *knew* he was busy—that his diary was jam-packed—but surely even Prince Regents were allowed a holiday sometimes?

' Of course you're busy.' She swallowed. 'You're always busy. I'm sorry. It was a stupid assumption for me to make.'

Something in the resigned tone of her voice stayed him, and he came up behind her, his fingers slipping to her bare shoulders and beginning to massage them. 'No, it was an easy assumption to make…but there aren't going to be any holidays, *bella*—at least, not for a while.'

'Oh, well,' she said brightly. 'I guess it'll be all the better when it happens.'

Frowning, he felt the tight tension in her shoulders as he attempted to explain something of his dilemma—he who had never had to offer anyone an explanation in his life. 'Taking over a monarchy like this is a bit like being brought in to head up a powerful organisation—except much of this I cannot delegate, because the buck stops with me. And yet because, ultimately, mine is only a *substitute* authority, I must run every decision past the government to ensure that I am acting in the country's best interests. *Porca miseria*—but your muscles are tight, *mia bella*.' Gold seared into aquamarine as their eyes locked in the looking glass. 'Perhaps I should take you to bed and help you relax in a way which would please us both,' he said softly.

For a moment, she allowed herself to dream. 'Wouldn't that be lovely?' she whispered.

His hand slipped beneath her gown to tease a nipple between thumb and forefinger, a smile curving his lips as he felt its immediate response. 'Mmm. It would be *perfetto*.'

She felt like a child who had been offered an ice cream, only to discover that the store had just closed. 'But…but there isn't time, is there?' she said, jerking away from the temptation of his touch. 'Not with forty people waiting to have dinner with us.'

Reality intruded like a cold shower—washing away the soft heat which always suffused his skin when she was near. What a distraction she was, with her pale hair and her trembling lips and that way she had of looking up at him. Swallowing down his frustration, Xaviero said something harsh and raw in Greek—in a tone she had never heard him use before—and Cathy held his gaze as she put her hairbrush down, with a hand which wasn't quite steady.

'Why don't you say it in English so at least I can understand?'

His mouth hardened. 'You don't want to hear it.'

'Oh, I think I do. Aren't wives supposed to know what's troubling their husbands, even if they're Prince Regents?' she questioned, her heart suddenly beginning to thump with a cold dread which made the palms of her hands grow clammy. 'And…and something is troubling you, isn't it, Xaviero?'

There was a split second of a pause. Because didn't articulating something make it real? And yet if he didn't tell someone he thought he just might explode. He shrugged, and then let out a ragged sigh. 'I just said how much I hate this life.'

Quietly spoken, his words ripped through her:

...how much I hate this life. Powerful words which laid bare a dissatisfaction she had suspected from the moment she'd arrived on the island. Was she implicated in that unhappiness? she wondered painfully. *Yet how could she not be—for wasn't she part of the whole package?*

'Anything specific?' she questioned, in a light tone. The kind of tone she'd once used to ask people if they'd like an extra blanket or not.

'Oh, I don't know—*everything*.' The words left his mouth with soft, explosive savagery, a torrent he'd been trying to deny for too long—even to himself. 'I hate it all. The demands. The lack of freedom and privacy. The way that everyone wants something from you. Everybody has a damned agenda.'

'But surely that was always the case? You've been royal all your life, Xaviero.'

'Only when I had to be.' He lifted his hand up to rake it back through the ebony hair, the light glinting off the pale gold of his crested cufflink. 'Why do you think I went to live in New York, where I was able to live a reasonably anonymous life? Because I didn't want to stand out. It's why I picked the isolation of the countryside, when I decided to settle in England.'

'Then this happened, out of the blue,' she said slowly, praying that his valet or her lady-in-waiting wouldn't come in and disturb them—because Xaviero had never talked to her like this before. 'And there was absolutely nothing you could do about it.'

'No. My fate has been sealed,' he said, with an air of finality, and then his face darkened. 'And yet I have no right to express any kind of dissatisfaction with my lot. How can I—when my brother is lying insensible in what seems like a cruel enactment of our mother's demise? And if I'm honest—really honest—weren't there times in our childhood when I *wanted* the monarchy? When I wished it was *me* being prepared for the kingdom, not Casimiro. What is it that they say,' he added bitterly. *'Be careful what you wish for.'*

Cathy flinched, praying for the right words as she saw the deepening of the painful lines etched in his face. Something which could lessen his grief and his guilt and might make him see the positives in a life he would never have chosen for himself. Couldn't she persuade him that together they could learn a different way of living—if he was prepared to give it a try? But before she could speak, there was a gentle tap on the door and Xaviero opened it himself to find one of the butlers standing there.

Black eyebrows were arched in impatient query. '*Yes*, what is it?'

'Highness, your guests have arrived.'

Xaviero nodded, wishing for a brief and crazy moment that he were back in her tiny cottage, sitting in the soft, scented oasis of her garden, drinking wine from those ridiculous cheap little tumblers she used to use. But there was no use yearning for the impossible—because hadn't he learnt by now that duty always came first? And how could he expect Cathy to adhere to that principle if he found he was trying to shirk it himself? 'We'll be right down.' He turned to her. 'Ready?'

'Yes.' She hesitated. 'Xaviero, there must be something you could—'

'Forget it.' Although soft, his tone was emphatic. 'It doesn't matter.'

She wanted to say that it *did*—but her heart sank as she saw the now familiar cool mask back in place and she sensed his confidences of just a moment ago already being erased from his mind. And yet his disclosures—far from bringing her closer to him—had left her feeling distinctly unsettled. Insecurity flooded through her as she realised she hadn't been imagining his frustration at his life here at all. And what would happen if that frustration built and built?

Side by side they walked into the ante-room where the assembled guests were waiting and Cathy carefully composed her face to prepare herself for the inevitable scrutiny. She was used to this by now—the way the women always looked her over and sized her up, as if trying to decide whether she was fit to be married to such a devastatingly handsome and eligible prince.

This was the part of the evening where she and Xaviero again went their separate ways—she to chat to the wives of the visiting delegation and to sip at a glass of water. She had given up taking wine before or during the meal—it made her grow too pink and uninhibited and sometimes she had to bite back things she really wanted to say.

It's as much a prison for me as it is for Xaviero, she realised suddenly as they were led into dinner, to opposite ends of the formally decorated table.

She watched Xaviero during the meal, her eyes straying to him despite her determination to respond enthusiastically to the man seated next to her. From time to time he would look up, his golden eyes sparking out a silent question—occasionally, he would even toss her a slow smile. And Cathy was aware that she seized on these little crumbs of affection as a starving dog would a piece of meat.

She saw the sultry woman at his side slant him a beguiling smile—and, to be fair to Xaviero, he didn't respond to it at all. No telltale silent flirtation in return. But that was because they were newly-weds—when she was still completely captivating to him in the bedroom and he couldn't seem to get enough of her. What would happen when that wore off—as people always said it did?

Trapped within the confines of their largely separate lives—might not Xaviero choose to dabble a little elsewhere, as royal men throughout history had been inclined to do? The opportunity was always there for them—they could have their pick of women so eager to bed a prince that discretion would be guaranteed. Why, didn't weak and ambitious men sometimes even offer up their wives as some kind of noble sexual sacrifice?

Maybe that was another reason why he had chosen a compliant wife—one so grateful to be married to him that she would put up with just about anything. Was he expecting her to turn a blind eye to his indiscretions as royal wives were famous for doing? She shuddered, quickly putting her heavy fork down before she did something unforgivable—like dropping it on one of the porcelain plates.

But it was like finding a tiny tear in an old dress and poking your finger inside it—only to discover that you were making the hole much bigger. It was as if tonight had opened the floodgates on all the inadequacies in their relationship—or had Xaviero's own words of dissatisfaction about his life helped to crystallise her own?

We've never even talked about children, she realised. Quickly, she gulped down a mouthful of water and felt it refresh her parched lips, but underneath the table her knees were trembling. Xaviero had continued to use protection after their marriage and she hadn't even questioned it—just tacitly accepted it as she had done so much else. Oh, she was certainly compliant! Did he *want* children? And could she bring children into this kind of peculiar marriage—or was this a 'normal' marriage in the royal world?

I'll ask him, she thought—though a wave of dark misery swept over her. *I'll ask him tonight.*

Dessert appeared—an extravagant confection of lemon cream and spun sugar—and Cathy was eyeing it unenthusiastically when one of Xaviero's aides entered the room and went immediately over to his side to speak softly in the Prince's ear.

Even without her crash-course in protocol, Cathy would have known that it was rare indeed for the Prince Regent to be interrupted when he was in the middle of an official dinner. And rarer still for Xaviero to suddenly rise to his feet, his face growing ashen.

Something was wrong. Helplessly, her fingers clutched at her napkin. She wanted to ask him what was happening but, of course, she couldn't do that for he wouldn't dream of telling her before an audience.

And then another aide entered and Xaviero quickly joined him at the side of the room, bending his dark head as the man spoke in a low, urgent tone in his ear. By now all the guests had abandoned any pretence at continuing with their dinner—as everyone seemed to sense that something momentous was happening.

What the hell was going on?

Xaviero's face grew suddenly taut as he spoke in a low voice to the assembled company. 'I regret to say that urgent matters of state mean that my wife and I must now leave you,' he said, and then paused before the golden eyes seared into her. 'Catherine, you will please join me?'

It felt like a summons, it most definitely *was* a summons, and never had a walk seemed so long as Cathy found her feet and slowly walked down the long dining room towards him. Searching his face for some sort of clue for the reasons behind this extraordinary break with protocol, she found none. Just a bleak and unfathomable countenance, but then, wasn't that Xaviero all over—because since when had she ever been able to read anything in his shuttered face?

In silence, they left the room—the aides following at a discreet distance—and once they were out of earshot of the assembled dignitaries she turned to him in perplexity.

'Xaviero, what on earth is going on?'

He seemed to struggle to find the right words. 'The hospital has just rung—'

Her heart missed a beat as she held her breath, sensing tragedy. 'And?'

He swallowed. 'My brother has tonight awakened from his coma.'

CHAPTER ELEVEN

THE car drove them straight to the hospital—but Cathy was still reeling from her husband's shock announcement and his inexplicably bleak response to it.

'I thought…I thought you'd be overjoyed about your brother's recovery, and yet…' she said slowly, registering the sombre set of his features in the dimmed light of the limousine. 'What exactly have they told you?'

'That he suddenly opened his eyes and began to speak. They're running tests now—but they say…' His voice thickened. 'They say he's going to make a full recovery.'

'So why…?' Dared she? *Dared* she? 'Why your restrained response?'

'I'll believe it when I see it for myself,' he said harshly as the car drew up outside the brightly lit and modern hospital, where the medical director was waiting for them.

The news was good. In fact, the news was pretty unbelievable, Cathy thought as she sat in the big, airy office and listened while the doctor explained that every test they'd run had been favourable. That every system was functioning and that the King was demanding physiotherapy as soon as possible because he wanted to—as the doctor relayed with the hint of a smile—'get the hell out of here'.

Xaviero felt a pulse working at his temple. 'That sounds like Casimiro. So when can I see him?'

'I can take you to him now, Your Highness.'

He turned to her, but the golden eyes were shadowed, distracted. 'Come, Catherine.'

Cathy was suddenly acutely aware that she was dressed in a scarlet evening gown—even though her shoulders were covered in a pashmina which had been thrust at her by an aide before their hasty departure. And aware too that her presence

was superfluous to what would—and should—
be an emotional reunion between the two
brothers. She shook her head. 'No. Better that
you see him alone,' she said quietly.

Eyebrows arrowed together in a frown.
'You're sure?'

'Quite sure.'

She sat drinking coffee while she waited, unable
to stop the stream of thoughts pouring into her
mind—no matter how much she tried to stop them.
But shamefully the one which dominated all others
was purely selfish. And while Cathy's heart felt fit
to burst for joy that the young King should have
come back to life, she wouldn't have been human
if a deep dark wave of fear hadn't washed over her.

Because my place here is now redundant.

Xaviero didn't need her any more. He didn't
need a wife by his side to ease the burden of
unwanted duty thrust upon him by circumstance.
He didn't even need to be here himself—not now.
Judging by what the doctor had told them, the
King was well on the way to recovery and would
soon resume his rightful place on the throne.

She was so caught up in her troubled thoughts that when Xaviero appeared in the doorway for a moment she scarcely recognised him. Because this was a man she had never seen before—one transformed by a sudden sense of joy. It was as if he had been carrying around with him an impossibly heavy burden—and someone had suddenly lifted it from his shoulders and the weight had vanished. He was free, she thought—with another shiver of foreboding.

'How…how is he?' she asked.

'It's *unbelievable*.' Xaviero expelled a ragged sigh—because hadn't the past come back to haunt him as he had stood beside his brother's bed? Didn't he know better than anyone that doctors sometimes raised hopes when those hopes were better to let wither, and die? But the spectre of his mother's own failed recovery had been banished by the first sight of his brother's smile. 'He's…'

He had been about to say that Casimiro was the same as he'd ever been, but that would be a lie. His brother had changed—Xaviero had sensed that from the moment he had walked into the intensive care unit. And when you stopped to think about it an experience like that was bound to change you profoundly—for didn't death's dark shadow throw the rest of your life into focus and force you to reevaluate it?

'He's going to be okay,' he said, in a shaky voice which didn't sound like his own voice.

Her own fears forgotten, Cathy went to him then—putting her arms very tightly around him and resting her head against his shoulder, breathing in the raw masculine scent that was all his.

'Oh, Xaviero,' she whispered. 'I'm so very happy for you. So happy for him.'

'Not as happy as I'm feeling right now,' he whispered, his arms snaking round her waist as he buried his face in the silken tumble of her hair.

The car took them back to the palace, and, after telling the assembled staff the news, they hurried to their suite with matched and urgent steps. Xaviero was on fire, and so was she—he barely waited until the door was shut before impatiently sliding the soft silk-satin up over her hips.

Questing fingers found her searing heat and he didn't even bother to remove the delicate lace panties—just hurriedly thrust the panel aside, as he unzipped and freed himself and pushed her back against the wall.

Cathy gasped as she felt the tip of him nudging intimately against her—wanting to squirm her hips to accommodate him—longing to feel his hard power filling her and completing her. But as he prepared to thrust into her—it was she who realised what was about to happen. Who cried out a little protest before firmly pushing against his chest before it was too late—before he risked trapping himself again, only this time by something which was preventable.

'C-c-contraception!' she gasped out.

Xaviero's mouth hardened as he haltingly complied with her wishes—the mood not exactly broken, but certainly changed by her shuddered command. And something in the act of putting the barrier between them distilled some of the jubilant wildness which had been heating his blood. His thrust was still deep, but his movements were more measured. Instead of the fiery, fast consummation he had sought, he now controlled the pace almost cold-bloodedly—nearly bringing her to fulfilment over and over again until at last she sobbed out his name in a helpless kind of plea.

Only then did he let go, feeling her convulse about him before allowing his own—strangely bittersweet—orgasm to follow. Afterwards he carried her over to the bed and ripped the silk gown from her body—thus ensuring she would never wear it again, for its associations were now too strongly linked to powerful emotions he would prefer not to remember.

It was a long and erotic night. He made love to her over and over again and, even while Cathy revelled in the incredible sensations he evoked in her, it felt almost as if he were trying to prove a point. What point was that? she wondered distractedly. To establish that he could reduce her to boneless longing any time he wanted to?

She woke to find him already dressed, and realised that it was the first time she had seen him in jeans since she'd arrived on the island. It was a strange moment—as memories fused and became tangled. It reminded her of the first time she'd seen him, when she had been crazily convinced that he was an itinerant worker!

Was he dressing down and reverting to the old Xaviero now that he had been freed from the burden of responsibility? And were his shadowed eyes an acknowledgement that perhaps he had been a little too hasty in acquiring a bride—that maybe he should have waited a little longer before encumbering himself?

She sat up in bed, pushing back her tousled hair—aware of the aching deep inside her body and the soft glow of her flesh. 'You're—you're up early.'

Golden eyes flicked over her. 'An emergency meeting of the government has been called.' The sight of her rosy-tipped breasts was making him want to tumble her back down among the already-rumpled sheets and Xaviero walked over to the safe distance of the window. 'We have to discuss what kind of statement we need to issue to the press,' he added tersely.

'Oh. I see.' He was standing in the shadows—she could barely read the expression on his face, but that wasn't such a new thing, was it? Wasn't his face fathomless even in brightest sunshine—the man who never gave anything of himself away? *Tell him now. Tell him while you have the courage.* 'Xaviero…this…changes everything.'

'I know it does.'

His instant confirmation added yet another brick to the fast-building realisation that what they had between them was as fragile as one of those flowers which bloomed in the desert. Glorious for one short day—and then gone for ever.

'You won't want to stay on the island once Casimiro is fully recovered.'

'I think I might cramp his style somewhat,' he observed drily, and sent her a sarcastic glance. 'Don't you?'

Don't be swayed by that glimpse of mocking humour, she told herself fiercely as she pulled a silken nightgown over her head—feeling less vulnerable now that her nakedness was hidden. *Concentrate on what is real and what is not. You can't trap him—it isn't fair. And you can't hold him to a union which was made in haste for all the wrong reasons. So set him free, Cathy. If you really love him—you'll give him his liberty.*

'I think we should dissolve the marriage,' she said bluntly.

Perhaps it was the shock of a woman actually suggesting they *end* it which surprised him more than anything—for Xaviero had never been dumped by anyone. But an innate sense of his own self-worth meant that he couldn't quite believe it. He stared at her with a sense of growing disbelief in his eyes. 'You want that?' he queried incredulously.

She remembered what he had said to her just yesterday, when she had been dressing for dinner. *How I hate this life.* Well, now he didn't have to live it any more, did he?

'I think it would be for the best,' she answered carefully, praying that her voice wouldn't tremble and give her away. 'You've just said you aren't going to want to stay here.' The face he presented her was a cold, dark mask as she strove to make him understand. 'So what will happen? Imagine it, Xaviero. You'll go to South America to look at polo ponies as planned—taking with you a wife you only married because you envisaged that circumstances would be entirely different? And then what? You return to Colbridge and start up your polo school with the hotel all tarted up and me, the ex-chambermaid installed as its new chatelaine? Come on—it's a crazy idea. Laughable. Why, the press would have a field-day!'

He couldn't deny the essential truth in her words but what struck him was how ironic life could be. How determined and how level-headed her argument! His compliant little chambermaid sounding so quietly confident as she told him that their marriage should be dissolved. *Her* telling *him*?

Pride made him shrug, telling himself that it was ego causing this sharp pierce of blistering pain. What did she think he was about to do—start begging her to stay? Had she overdeveloped a sense of her own importance since she'd been using the title 'Princess' before her name? Well, she would soon learn another lesson—that Xaviero di Cesere was dependent on no woman!

He nodded. 'We'll need to think about how best to go about it.' Dark lashes shaded the golden gleam of his eyes as he set his lips in a cynical line. 'In fact, I'm wondering if maybe we might be able to bury the story in the good news about Casimiro's recovery.'

Didn't part of her crumple then, because hadn't she—against all the odds—been holding out for more? All he had needed to do was to show her *something*—some sign that she meant more to him than compliance and passion. But there was nothing. That icy inaccessibility was back and all that concerned her husband was the most diplomatic way to announce their divorce to the press!

'Perhaps you could let me know what you decide is best,' she said as she pushed aside the sheets and got out of bed. 'I'll stay on the island for as long as you think I should—though, obviously, I'd prefer it if that time was as short as possible.'

'*Obviously,*' he echoed sarcastically, but the sight of the buttery fabric clinging to her voluptuous curves was a temptation beyond endurance and he swiftly turned his back and slammed his way out of the bedroom.

CHAPTER TWELVE

'CASIMIRO wants to see you.'

Cathy looked up from where she'd been studying the drawer lined with soft pastel piles of silk lingerie and debating how many of the sensual little sets she could reasonably take back to England with her. Or maybe she should leave the whole lot behind. Wouldn't it be easier that way? Easier to forget…

'Cathy?' Xaviero's voice cut into her thoughts. 'Did you hear what I said?'

Sitting back on her heels, Cathy forced a smile. 'He wants to see *me*? Why?'

Xaviero's mouth hardened. 'How the hell should I know? I'm not privy to his thoughts. He just said he'd like to see you before you leave.'

'Oh, right.'

Xaviero glanced at his watch. 'Everything's all been arranged. A car will be here to pick you up just after two. If there are any problems, then just speak to Flavia.'

She stared at him. 'You mean…you mean, you aren't going to *be* here?'

'To wave you off as the car drives away?' His lips curved into a cynical smile. 'No, Cathy, I am not. I don't do goodbyes—I don't find them particularly palatable.'

Who did? She swallowed down the sudden lump which had risen in the back of her throat along with the telltale taste of tears. 'So…so this is *it*?'

'Yes, this is it,' he said implacably, doing his best to ignore the bright glitter of tears in her eyes which made them look as blue as a Californian swimming pool. 'This is what you wanted.'

'What I thought was best.'

'And you're right,' he agreed steadily. 'It is. Every single reason you gave as to why we shouldn't be together made perfect sense. And there are positives, of course. You'll leave this marriage a considerably wealthy woman—'

'I *don't want* your damned money!'

'Well, you're going to get it whether you like it or not! No ex-wife of mine is going to go back to being a chambermaid!' he bit out.

'You can't stop me!'

'No,' he concurred. 'I can't. What you do when you leave here is up to you. You're on your own. But what I can do is to make over a house and an income for you to do with as you see fit—because I will not be accused of having married a woman and then leaving her in penury!'

Cathy closed her eyes. Of course. This was all about *image*, wasn't it? And ego. *His* ego. How he would be perceived and judged by the rest of the world. If ever she had needed convincing that her decision was wise, he had just reinforced it with that damage-limitation statement of his.

'Now you'd better go to see Casimiro,' he continued, hardening his heart to the sudden chalky whiteness of her face. 'He may be grateful to be alive, but his old monarchical attitude has set in—and he doesn't like to be kept waiting.'

'So this really is *goodbye*?' Her voice was a tremulous little whisper, the realisation driving a sharp twist of pain through her heart.

'Yes, Cathy—it really is.'

His hand reached out—and for one moment Cathy thought that he might be about to pull her into his arms. And if he did that—she would be lost. Completely lost. As lost as she had been when he'd proposed this farce of a marriage. *So do it*, her eyes begged him silently. *Make me feel you need me.*

Instead, he merely caught hold of her own inert fingers and slowly brought them up to his lips—his mouth brushing against their unmoving tips in a parody of courtly manners. She could feel the warmth of his breath and could do nothing to stop the involuntary shudder of longing which shivered its way down her spine.

'Goodbye, Cathy.' Their eyes met in a long moment and then he let her go. 'Now run along and find the King,' he said softly.

Somehow she managed to leave the room without stumbling—but the tears had started spilling down her cheeks and she took a couple of moments' refuge in one of the out-of-the-way cloakrooms before she dared head for the King's quarters.

A quick glance in the mirror at her deathly pale face and the shadows beneath her eyes bore testimony to the strain she'd been living under in the days since Casimiro's recovery.

During Casimiro's convalescence, her husband had spent much of his time with his brother—being close to hand as the King's health and strength had rapidly returned. He had also been making arrangements to travel to South America—and for a trust to be set up in Cathy's name, as well as a house in London which was to be hers. Her threats to immediately sell the pretty Georgian property and donate all the money to charity had been met with a careless shrug.

'I don't care *what* you do with it,' he had drawled.

And why should he? Her decision to leave had been made and Xaviero had accepted it. In fact, to Cathy's horror, he seemed to have compartmentalised her—it was as if she were already in his past. As if she had ceased to exist.

Only in bed at night was there a temporary type of truce when they came together for some pretty explosive sex. And, while Cathy had no real experience of other men, she had learned enough to realise that they viewed sex in an entirely different way from women. Xaviero could still enjoy her body and give her delirious amounts of enjoyment in return—it didn't actually *mean* anything, not to him. Whereas for *her*…

For her it was something else entirely. Every poignant and exquisite caress entranced her. As she gasped out her orgasm beneath his hard, powerful body she was haunted by the terrible knowledge that she would never know pleasure like this again. But she also knew that deep down her reasons for leaving were sound—and that Xaviero had made no attempt to talk her out of them.

Brushing the last rogue tear from her eye and realising that she was keeping the King waiting, Cathy hurried from the cloakroom to his offices at the far end of the palace, where an aide showed her straight in. Casimiro was seated at a huge desk and he looked up as she walked in.

'Catherine,' he murmured. 'At last.'

She sank into a deep curtsey. 'I'm sorry I'm late—'

'It isn't something which happens very often,' he said drily. 'Come in, and sit down.'

She slid onto the seat opposite him and, even though it was probably discourteous to stare at the monarch, Cathy simply couldn't help herself. Because his recovery was like a miracle. Like something you might see in a film but could never imagine happening in real life. The pale and unmoving figure who had been hooked up to all those wires and tubes in Intensive Care was now looking as vital and as vibrant as life itself.

The ebony hair, which had been shaved during his time in hospital, was fast growing back, showing the hint of a recalcitrant wave. Regular exposure to the sun meant that his olive skin had lost its pallor and now glowed with good health. He had been receiving physiotherapy, too—and had hit the gym with his trainer, so that lean muscle had returned to bulk out a fairly formidable physique.

He was an amazingly handsome man who looked, Cathy thought, very like Xaviero. But Casimiro's eyes were a much darker gold than his brother's and, curiously, his lips—although innately arrogant—were not nearly as cynical.

'So, Catherine,' he said, in a voice which sounded faintly amused. 'You study the King very intently today. What is your verdict?'

'You are looking very well, Your Majesty.'

He smiled. 'And I am feeling very well,' he said in a satisfied voice before his eyes narrowed and his voice grew thoughtful. 'Such praise is praise indeed from you, who saw me at my very sickest.' He looked at her and gave a soft sigh. 'You know I have a duty to thank you.'

'You don't have to thank me, Your Majesty.'

'Oh, but I do,' he demurred, his voice now underpinned with a stubborn quality which reminded Cathy painfully of Xaviero. 'The doctors don't know why I came out of the coma—and perhaps they never will—but they said I should never underestimate the healing power of another human voice. And your voice was the one I heard most of all during my time in hospital.' His voice grew even more thoughtful. 'In fact, the only one I heard so consistently.'

'Well, Xaviero was too busy with affairs of state—'

'How faithfully you defend him!' he murmured. 'And women are better at talking than men. Yes, he told me.'

For some stupid reason, Cathy found herself blushing. 'He told you that?'

'Yes.'

There was an unmistakable question in his dark gold eyes but Cathy clamped her lips tightly closed and knotted her fingers together in her lap. The last thing she wanted to do was to break down and dissolve into tears in front of the King.

'Catherine, why are you leaving?'

She swallowed. *Act normal. Stay calm.* 'Because there is no need for me to stay now that you are returned to health, Your Majesty. You have resumed your rightful place on the throne and Xaviero will soon be leaving the island.'

'That wasn't what I mean and you know it,' he said.

Cathy could hear the impatience in his voice, but it wasn't really his place to get impatient, was it? 'Wasn't it?'

For a moment he studied her impassive face. 'Xaviero told me how you met,' he said suddenly.

'He…he did?'

'He did. He said he was playing at being ordinary. It was something he used to do all the time when we were younger—a game he used to play.'

Cathy swallowed. A *game*? 'Really?'

'Yes.' His eyes narrowed and he leaned back in his gilded chair, the fingertips of each hand meeting to form a spire. 'You know, most people think that the younger son always has it easy.'

He was looking at her as if he wanted her to make some kind of comment and Cathy shrugged. 'But not when you're royal, I suppose?'

'No. Not when you're royal. It's the heir who

always gets the attention. My father spent most of his time with me—instructing me about my inheritance—and Xaviero was pretty much left to his own devices. He was adored by our mother, of course.'

Casimiro paused for a moment and this time Cathy said nothing.

'Nobody told Xaviero just how sick she was,' he continued slowly. 'They led him to believe that she would recover. I think it was the way they dealt with children back then—never acknowledging the darker side of life. He wasn't even allowed to go to the funeral—it was decided that it would be too distressing for him. And after her death, my father turned all his attention on grooming me to succeed him, so that in a way it was as if Xaviero had lost both parents.'

Cathy bit her lip. 'Why…why are you telling me all this?'

'Because you told me about your life while I lay in a coma, Catherine…and some of those words have remained fixed in my mind—they must have done, else how would I have known them when

I awoke?' His mouth curved into a fleeting smile. 'About your tenants and your beautiful garden in England. The same garden in which you and Xaviero used to sit on long summer evenings and drink wine from cheap glasses.'

'But I didn't tell you about *that*,' she breathed.

'No. Xaviero did. My brother and I have talked long and often since my recovery.'

She stared at him. 'I don't understand where this is going,' she whispered.

'Don't you? Listen, Catherine.' Casimiro leaned forward, the spire dismantled as he placed his palms on the desk, almost in a gesture of supplication. 'If you were prepared to go to him. To seek his understanding and explain that you acted with undue haste in telling him you wanted to leave. If you were suitably contrite…' there was a moment's pause '…then I think he may be prepared to give you a second chance.'

Cathy froze. 'Excuse me?'

'I think he may be prepared to overlook your—'

'No!' She felt the colour blanch from her

cheeks as she saw his startled expression, but suddenly she didn't care if her interruption had been an outrageous breach of protocol. 'I am not having this conversation,' she said, in a low voice. 'Has Xaviero picked you out as some sort of broker—to say to me what he hasn't got the nerve to say himself? To ask me to make some kind of unnecessary apology in order to pander to his pride?'

'He doesn't know *what* I'm saying,' Casimiro ground out.

'Well, my mind is made up.' Because a lot of people had dud childhoods in some sort of way, didn't they? But that didn't mean they should behave like emotional ice cubes for the rest of their lives. And deep down Cathy knew that it didn't matter what Casimiro said. The only person who might have persuaded her to stay was his brother—and he had walked away as if her going had meant nothing to him. Because *she didn't mean anything to him*. And it wasn't enough. It wasn't enough now—and time would only make it worse. The balance of love was completely unequal—and she could not imprison him in a marriage which was no longer necessary. She would be living on tenterhooks, waiting for him to tire of her—before seeking a royal mistress and leaving his grieving and unloved wife at home. She rose to her feet. 'I'm sorry.'

'So you are both as proud and as stubborn as each other!' Casimiro snapped.

'So it would seem,' said Cathy. 'And now I must beg your leave, Your Majesty. The car will be arriving for me shortly. I am so happy that you are well again, sire.' Her voice wavered a little at this. 'And I wish you a long and glorious reign.'

With this she gave a quick curtsey before hurrying back to her rooms, but inside she could feel a mixture of anger and indignation bubbling up. The King expected her to go and seek forgiveness from his brother, but for what? For trying to love a man who had no love to give her in return.

Her hands were trembling as she threw a few ill-chosen items of clothing in her case before slamming it shut, but at least the fury she now felt helped dull some of the pain.

But there was no formal line-up of staff as she went down the sweeping marble staircase into the lavishly tiled marble entrance hall. Just Flavia, whose own smile of farewell was as cool as if Cathy had been introduced to her only minutes before. But Flavia was an aide who had spent all her life defusing emotion—because that was what royal life demanded of its players. Cathy knew that. It was the downside to all the jewels and fawning. *And I never wanted that*, she told herself fiercely. *All I ever wanted was Xaviero—and he comes at too high a price.*

Outside sat the limousine, its powerful engine giving a soft roar of life when she appeared, and Cathy gave one last look around the beautiful courtyard, trying to imprint it on her memory. The succulent plants. The bright, fragrant blooms. The fountain which plumed out its rainbow spray. And always the bright blue sky and soft heat of the sun—as golden as the eyes of a man she would never forget.

Grateful for the sunglasses which shielded her

brimming eyes, Cathy slid into the back seat as the car pulled away. She could just sink back into its air-conditioned luxury and say nothing until they reached the airfield and the plane which would take her back to England.

And then?

She didn't know and, at this moment, she didn't particularly care. She felt like a small animal which had wandered into a trap and escaped with wounds which might never heal.

Painfully, she watched the city walls retreating, the wide roads leading to the airport growing suddenly narrower, and she frowned. The driver was obviously taking a different route from the one by which she'd arrived.

She didn't know when exactly it was that she began to get alarmed—maybe when the car began to bump its way up a dusty road which looked as if it led to nowhere, and then stopped completely. What was going on?

Pressing the intercom connecting her with the driver, she found herself hoping that he spoke English—though surely even with her rudimentary Italian she could manage to convey that she was supposed to be catching a plane.

'*Scusi, signor...*' But then the words died on her lips as she saw the driver getting out of the car and opening her door. This was completely unprecedented! Her heart gave a leap of fear—and then a leap of something else entirely as she removed her dark shades. Because he was now pulling off the peaked cap which had hidden his ebony hair and shaded the remarkable gleam of his golden eyes.

And she found herself looking into the oddly forbidding face of her husband.

CHAPTER THIRTEEN

'XAVIERO!' Cathy gasped out. 'What…what on earth are you doing here?'

Dropping his chauffeur's cap into the dust, he moved towards her with sinuous grace. 'I am stopping us both from making the biggest mistake of our lives.'

'You mean you're playing another of your games of pretending to be ordinary? Today, a driver—tomorrow, who knows? A painter and decorator again?'

'This is no game—this is the real thing.' But a note of admiration had entered his voice. How feisty she was! 'My brother is still reeling from the fact that you marched out of his office without being given permission! He said that it was the most imperiously royal gesture he had ever witnessed!' His golden eyes raked over her face as if he had never quite seen it before. 'Oh, Cathy, what have I done?' he groaned, and then pulled her into his arms and started to kiss her.

For several sweet moments she gave into that kiss, feeling herself begin to melt beneath its sensual onslaught before summoning up every ounce of power she possessed to tear her mouth away from his and to push uselessly at his chest. 'Don't,' she whispered. 'Just don't.'

Something in the defeated little tone of her voice stilled him. 'But you want me to.'

Frustratedly, she shook her head. 'Of course I want you to! I've always wanted you to—that's been part of the problem. But the attraction I feel for you has blinded me to the truth. And it's no good, Xaviero. Not any more.'

Lifting a finger, he caught hold of a bright golden strand of hair which had fallen over her eyes and pushed it away from her flushed face. 'Why not?' he questioned softly.

'Because it's just…just sex.'

'I thought you liked sex.'

'You know I do.' She looked up at him. 'But it's not enough. I thought it could be, but it can't. You wanted me compliant—and maybe I was, but not any more. I seem to have changed—when you think about it, I suppose it was inevitable I would. And I can't just *be* what you want me to be—not any more. Can't you see that? I am not the same person. I'm no longer just someone you can mould—so I no longer fit the bill of what you really want from a wife.'

Xaviero's heart twisted and his breath felt hot and harsh in his throat. He knew what she wanted from him—but couldn't she at least meet him halfway? Because there was a sense that if he let go—really let go—and told her what he knew deep down she needed to know, he would make himself weak in the process. That he would lay himself open to all that terrible pain he'd experienced when he'd discovered that love made you vulnerable.

And yet, did he really have an alternative? Because hadn't the pain of knowing that she was going to walk out of his life been more than he could bear? He had tried to ignore it and then to block it—but it had kept coming back at him like a persistent mosquito in the dead of night. Did he somehow think he was immune to all the emotional stuff that other people had to deal with—that he could get away with behaviour which would be tolerated simply because of his royal status? Yes, he did. And up until now, he always had.

But then he had discovered that, for all his pro-testations about wanting to be treated like any other man—the truth was that he wanted it both ways. All ways. That he donned the protection of his royal mantle whenever it suited him.

'And if I told you that I think I was fooling myself all along?' he grated. 'What then?'

'That kind of admission doesn't sound like the Xaviero *I* know,' she answered quietly.

'No. It doesn't feel like the Xaviero I know, either. Maybe you aren't the only one to have changed, Cathy.' He gave a short, bitter laugh. 'When I gave you that cold-blooded list of requirements for a wife I thought I was being completely honest with you—and I've since discovered that honest was the very last thing I was being.'

Cathy frowned. 'You mean you didn't want someone—'

'I mean that there were a million women out there who would have fitted the bill for a marriage of convenience—even at such short notice. Pure women. Aristocratic women. Heiresses who would have found royal life no great challenge. I could have picked up a list of my ex-lovers and any one of them would have come running.'

'But you didn't do that,' said Cathy slowly.

'No. That's right. I didn't. I chose the most unsuitable woman of all—but she was the one who happened to make me *feel* stuff. The one who provided an oasis of calm in her simple little home. The one who had wanted me just as much when I walked into the hotel covered in mud and sweat from a hard morning's riding as when she discovered who I really was.' He looked at her, his eyes full of question.

'Sometimes I wanted that man more,' she admitted. 'I wanted you without all the trouble of the trappings.'

'I know,' he said simply. 'And can you understand how much that means to me? To be wanted for who you are, rather than what you are? I've never had that before. It made me feel...*emotion*.' He shrugged his shoulders. 'And that's why I fought it, just like I'd fought it all my life.'

When, as a lonely and bereaved little boy, he had sought comfort in his horses. She pictured the isolated little figure he must have been—brave and handsome and lonely as hell. 'Xaviero,' she whispered.

'No.' His voice was husky, thick with emotion. 'Say nothing. Just hear me out. What I have given you and what I have offered you has not been enough—not nearly enough. In fact, it makes me ashamed to think of how little I was prepared to give you. I know you're not into jewels or palaces, or fast cars or fancy planes, but I wondered if there was something else which would win your heart and persuade you to stay with me?'

Cathy held her breath as she stared at him, her heart missing a beat as she dared not hope. But her fingernails dug painfully into her palms all the same. 'Th-that depends what you're offering,' she said shakily.

'I'm offering love,' he said simply. 'How does that sound?'

Cathy couldn't speak for the lump in her throat, trying to swallow it down, trying to tell herself he was still playing games with her. Yet the look of intensity blazing from the golden eyes suggested the very opposite—she had never seen such a blaze of burning emotion on Xaviero's face before. Those hard, stern features had softened into the expression of a man who was feeling something, who was calling out to her. And she felt the answering call of her own heart.

But she was scared. Too scared to clutch at something and then find that it had all been some ghastly mistake. And now she needed to be brave— because she could no longer hide behind *her* feelings, either. She needed to know exactly where she stood—and if the foundations weren't solid enough, then she would move on. 'L-love would be enough,' she said shakily. 'If…if it was meant.'

He drew a deep breath. He spoke three languages fluently, but in that moment he felt like a child uttering its first words. And he knew that he must make his intentions unmistakable, because this might be his last chance to hold onto the most precious thing in his life.

'I love you, Cathy,' he whispered. 'I love you so much that if you leave me now I don't know if I could bear it. I love you in a way I never thought I could love—and it's scaring the hell out of me.'

Xaviero *scared*? She looked into his golden eyes, and her heart turned over—because wasn't she scared herself? Terrified. Maybe it was the same for every couple who were teetering on the brink of love, no matter who they were or what their circumstances. Instinct told her to believe him—and something else reinforced that instinct. The same something which had brought her out to his Mediterranean island in the first place.

Faith. But not blind this time—because she

could read in his eyes the only thing she wanted from Xaviero. The only thing she had ever really wanted from him. Just love.

Her smile was tremulous but she was having to blink back the sudden onset of tears. The first time she had ever tasted the tears of joy.

'I believe you and I love you,' she said softly, and then her head fell to his shoulder and she began to cry.

EPILOGUE

THEY honeymooned in South America, where the lush green foothills of the Andes took Cathy's breath away. On a sleek white yacht which drifted from island to stunning island off the coast of Brazil, they basked in the sun and sipped caipirinhas as potent as they were delicious. And once, in glorious anonymity, they daringly tangoed on the streets of Buenos Aires, while their security mingled with the crowd, having nightmares.

Then they criss-crossed across vast sweeps of land to track down some of the very finest horses in the world. Cathy had decided that if she was going to live a fulfilled married life with her darling Xaviero—then she wanted to learn all about his passion.

Just as he wanted to learn about hers. For when they returned from their six-month idyll to England, it was to find the hotel transformed into a beautiful home—exquisite in every way except for one thing.

'They haven't touched the gardens!' said Cathy as she stared in dismay at weeds which had encroached even further onto the neglected flowerbeds.

'That's because I want you to redesign them,' said Xaviero softly.

'Me?'

'Absolutely you.'

'But I don't have any formal training,' Cathy protested.

His fingers tangled themselves in the golden silk of her hair. 'Maybe not—but you have a natural instinct and an eye for beauty which no amount of teaching could provide.' Briefly he touched his lips to hers. 'I want my polo school to offer scholarships to talented youngsters from all backgrounds, all over the world, Cathy. But I want more than to make them talented riders. I want to bring them here, where they can experience the kind of calm which you weave around you wherever you go. So create a beautiful oasis of a garden, my love,' he urged softly. 'A place where people can come and be at home with their senses.'

Cathy swallowed, dizzy with the sense of joy his words always provoked—words which pierced her heart with their beauty. Because with Xaviero's declaration of love for her, it seemed that a true poet had been liberated.

Even her projected scenario of the press mocking a chambermaid princess hadn't materialised. It seemed that she had struck some kind of chord and the world was delighted with the marriage. And despite her turning down countless interviews, there were abundant articles on what the magazines were calling 'The Cinderella Syndrome'. Cathy didn't mind a bit. She wanted all women to realise that anything was achievable. That it didn't matter who you were or where you came from—that love truly *could* conquer all.

From his new hotel in the south of France, Rupert had written a sycophantic letter offering them free use of the honeymoon suite—and Xaviero had given a shout of laughter as he'd hurled it straight into the bin.

Even Peter, now married and with his own little parish somewhere along the east coast of Scotland, had written offering his tentative congratulations and had mentioned that his church was badly in need of a replacement roof. And Cathy, feeling expansive, had sent him a cheque to pay for it and wished him every happiness in his new life.

Back on Zaffirinthos Casimiro was fully recovered and back at the helm, though seeing his brother's obvious joy had made him seem a little wistful.

'Perhaps he needs a Queen,' said Cathy hopefully and Xaviero laughed.

'You want the whole world to feel like we do, is that it, *mia tesoro*?'

She rose up on tiptoe and brushed her lips over his. 'Mmm. You think that's possible?'

'No,' he answered thickly, before pulling her closer. 'I don't. I think what we have is unique.'

And of course, it was. No two people were the same as them, nor ever would be. But to Cathy, Xaviero was not a prince or a world-class polo player or next in line to an island kingdom. He never had been. He was simply her man—her gorgeous golden-eyed man—and she loved him with every fibre of her being.

MILLS & BOON PUBLISH EIGHT LARGE PRINT TITLES A MONTH. THESE ARE THE EIGHT TITLES FOR MAY 2010.

❦

RUTHLESS MAGNATE, CONVENIENT WIFE
Lynne Graham

THE PRINCE'S CHAMBERMAID
Sharon Kendrick

THE VIRGIN AND HIS MAJESTY
Robyn Donald

INNOCENT SECRETARY… ACCIDENTALLY PREGNANT
Carol Marinelli

THE GIRL FROM HONEYSUCKLE FARM
Jessica Steele

ONE DANCE WITH THE COWBOY
Donna Alward

THE DAREDEVIL TYCOON
Barbara McMahon

HIRED: SASSY ASSISTANT
Nina Harrington

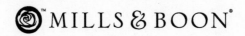

MILLS & BOON PUBLISH EIGHT LARGE PRINT TITLES A MONTH. THESE ARE THE EIGHT TITLES FOR JUNE 2010.

Cஐ

THE WEALTHY GREEK'S CONTRACT WIFE
Penny Jordan

THE INNOCENT'S SURRENDER
Sara Craven

CASTELLANO'S MISTRESS OF REVENGE
Melanie Milburne

THE ITALIAN'S ONE-NIGHT LOVE-CHILD
Cathy Williams

CINDERELLA ON HIS DOORSTEP
Rebecca Winters

ACCIDENTALLY EXPECTING!
Lucy Gordon

LIGHTS, CAMERA…KISS THE BOSS
Nikki Logan

AUSTRALIAN BOSS: DIAMOND RING
Jennie Adams